Saving Baby Doe

Also by Danette Vigilante:

The Trouble with Half a Moon

Danette Vigilante

G. P. Putnam's Sons

An Imprint of Penguin Group (USA)

G. P. Putnam's Sons
Published by the Penguin Group
Penguin Group (USA) LLC
375 Hudson Street
New York, NY 10014

USA | Canada | UK | Ireland | Australia
New Zealand | India | South Africa | China
penguin.com
A Penguin Random House Company

Library of Congress Cataloging-in-Publication Data
Vigilante, Danette.
Saving Baby Doe / Danette Vigilante.
pages cm
Summary: "When best friends Lionel and Anisa find and save an abandoned baby,
the fallout threatens to tear their relationship apart"—Provided by publisher.
[1. Best friends—Fiction. 2. Friendship—Fiction. 3. Foundlings—Fiction.
4. Single-parent families—Fiction. 5. Neighbors—Fiction. 6. Hispanic Americans—Fiction.
7. Conduct of life—Fiction.] I. Title.
PZ7.V6688Sav 2014 [Fic]—dc23 2013022728
Printed in the United States of America.
ISBN 978-0-399-25160-3
1 3 5 7 9 10 8 6 4 2

Design by Annie Ericsson.
Text set in Scherzo Std.

For Sal, because no matter the storm,
he never fails to keep me afloat.

And for my girls, Mia and Ami,
who make my world better.

It's early morning and the only noise she hears is the beat of her own heart. But she knows there is only one way the pain will end and she is more terrified than she's ever been.

Not even a blaring car horn fazes her as she struggles across the street. Once on the other side, she clings to a chain-link fence and gasps. She holds her breath as a wave of pain washes over her, squeezing at her belly unmercifully. Nine long torturous months filled with guilt is about to come to an end. She cannot give birth on the sidewalk for everyone to see. She cries out: *God help me.*

She locates an opening in the fence. Slowly making her way inside, she quickly spots a small trailer set up as an office. She tugs on the handle but her sweaty palm slips from the locked door. Panicked, she searches for a new place.

Another round of sharp, knifelike pain hits her and she instinctively squats. When the pain passes, she finds and enters a place where eyes cannot see what she's about to do. She locks the door and when the stabbing pain returns, she braces herself and begins to push . . .

1

When we come to the construction site where they're building a new grocery store, I'm reminded of how when I was little I had every kind of toy truck, tractor, and digger imaginable. If I could get into this site now, I'd be able to see what these machines are really like. I'd do some exploring too because there's a hole in the dirt that must go down deep, and maybe I'll even climb up to the door of the machine that says KOMATSU on the side. The one with a big digging arm in the front just like I used to have.

"Let's go in and check it out," I say, looking through the fence.

"No way, Lionel." Anisa's brown eyes stare at me in disbelief. "Are you crazy?"

"Why? Too chicken? Come on, let's just go see how deep that hole is. It's Sunday anyway, nobody's here."

Anisa points to a NO TRESPASSING sign. "Because I can read. Plus, last Sunday after church, I saw workers inside. Besides, doesn't your mother need milk? We're taking too long already."

I pull on the gate. Even though there's a fat chain holding it closed, a big space opens up. It's large enough for us to fit through.

"On a Sunday?" I search the site, looking for movement. "I don't see anyone now." I wait before giving her my best smile. "Come on, please?"

Anisa looks past me and into the site. "Papi used to work in places like this. He'd leave so early in the morning, we'd still be asleep . . ."

I nod, allowing Anisa to quietly remember her dad. I don't want her to be upset. After a minute I start to walk away. "That's okay, we don't have to go in. I'll come back another time. We should go."

"Wait," Anisa finally says, surprising me. "Let's do it, but too many people can see us going in this way."

"Really?"

"Yeah," she says, pointing to a spot across from us. "But it'll probably be better if we go in from over there."

"Yes!" I say as we hurry toward the other side of the construction site.

On the other side, part of the fence is broken and already pulled back. It's much easier to get in this way.

I take a good long look around, then slip inside. "Come on."

Instead of following, Anisa takes a step back and I'm afraid she might change her mind. "Don't worry, it'll be fine. You're wasting time."

It takes another minute before she comes in after me, and when she does, I tap her shoulder and yell, "You're it!" then take off.

I run past a small trailer, kicking up dust as I go.

"Hellooo? We're not seven years old!" Anisa says, taking her time.

Just before turning a corner, I say "Wow!" really loud, and before I know it, her long dark ponytail is swinging from side to side as she runs in my direction.

I slow down and pass six humongous machines facing all directions. It makes me think that once quitting time on Friday came, the workers jumped from the drivers' seats, leaving the big machines wherever they happened to be. There is no walkway or concrete. As far as I can see, the lot is made up of different-sized rocks, gravel, and mounds of dirt embedded with tracks from the equipment. The air is still and quiet except for my sneakers crunching the gravel. I imagine this is what the moon looks like. I close my eyes for a few seconds pretending to be an astronaut in space.

Big pieces of steel poke out of a deep wide hole. I stop to get a good look, then toss a rock into it, but it doesn't make much of a sound when it lands. "Come on," Anisa says. "I want to see if I can find the machine like Papi used to drive." She runs off before I can follow. I lose sight of her almost right away.

I hold my breath and run as fast as I can when I get to the Porta-Potties. I know the smell will be real bad.

Anisa's laughing from somewhere close. "Hey! Over here. What's taking you so long?"

"I'm coming, I'm coming!" I follow the sound of her voice.

She's scaling the side of a yellow machine that says CAT on the door when I catch up to her. "I think Papi worked in one like this."

I climb up after her. Together, we peer in through the window. There is only one leather seat covered in thick silver tape, two stick shifts, and two foot pedals. "Did he ever let you go inside one of these with him?"

She shakes her head. "You know, I keep his work boots underneath my bed. They still have dirt on them too. Is that weird?"

I think about my father, and wish he had died instead of leaving us by choice. At least if he'd died I'd know he didn't have a choice. I'm embarrassed to admit my wish to Anisa. "No, it's not." I watch our reflections through the window. Anisa's pretty, with an olive complexion and hair as dark and shiny as a coffee bean. I don't consider myself to be handsome. I think I look like Mr. Potato Head. I have the same coloring as one.

Anisa dries her eyes with the back of her hand. "We should go. We could probably get arrested for being here, you know," she says.

"For what? We're not doing anything."

Anisa starts to climb back down, then jumps the rest of the way. But her skirt tightens around her legs, making her leap too short. The edge of a metal beam slices her leg just before she lands on her hands and knees.

She squeezes her eyes shut. "Owww!"

I hurry after her. "Oh, no. Are you okay?"

"I got cut, and all because of this stupid thing," she says, pulling on the bottom part of her skirt.

It used to be that Anisa and her older sister, Eva, could wear whatever they wanted, but after their dad died and their mom started going to church, that all changed. Now they're not allowed to wear jeans or shorts or tank tops no matter how the weather is outside. I think that's crazy. As long as you're not out there showing off too much skin, it should be okay.

"Let me help you," I say, holding both hands out to her.

When she stands, blood runs down her leg. It's deep red and thick.

Every nerve in my body jumps to attention. "Yo, you're bleeding! I'm going to get help!" I'm already backing up.

"No! I'm okay. Look, it's nothing." She raises her skirt above the knee.

There's a long gash on her thigh. It runs almost down to her shin, showing pink flesh underneath. "It is too something. You might need stitches."

"No I don't." She bites her top lip. "It doesn't even hurt that much. Do you have something I can put on it?"

"Like what?" I say.

"I don't know! A tissue?"

All that blood is making me nervous. "Are you kidding? You need more than a tissue! We have to go."

Anisa pats the cut with her skirt. "Oooh, it burns."

"That's not helping. It's just smearing the blood around. Look, some of it dripped onto your feet."

"I guess we'd better go. I knew this was a bad idea."

She's right, but what's worse is that it was my idea. We should never have come in here. As we make our way back, Anisa is limping a little, so I let her lean on me.

"Maybe I'll need a tetanus shot."

"What's that?" I ask.

"Tetanus is a disease you can get when you're cut on something rusty," she says. "But there's a shot for it."

This is worse than I thought. "A disease?"

Anisa tries to smile but it's more of a grimace. "Calm down, I probably won't get it."

That doesn't make me feel better at all. Anisa might know about a lot of stuff but she doesn't know everything. If she does get sick because of this, I don't know what I'll do. All I know is we have to get out of here as fast as we can and get to a doctor. I try not to think about the trouble we're going to be in once we get home.

"You think you could walk a little quicker, especially when we get to those Porta-Potties?" I say. "You should hold your nose too."

When I was little, my father took me to the circus and I drank too many fruit punch slushies. I almost peed my pants. I was happy when my father said he found a bathroom, but when he brought me over to a plastic blue-and-white box the size of a refrigerator, I was confused.

"Where's the bathroom?" I asked.

He pointed to the Porta-Potti. "Right here."

"That's too small to be a bathroom."

He laughed and opened the door. A hot burst of stinky humid air swooshed out and hit us in the face. I've never smelled anything so bad in my whole life. It was worse than the monkey house at the Bronx Zoo and hard-boiled eggs mixed together. I covered my mouth and nose with both hands and ran away. Dad let me pee behind the temporary tattooing tent.

"Okay." Anisa's voice cracks.

Just then there's some kind of screeching in the distance. I don't think too much about it because Brooklyn is full of different noises.

"Hey, you hear that?" Anisa says. "Sounds like a cat. Maybe it needs help."

Anisa loves all animals but especially cats. She even volunteers at the animal shelter sometimes.

We stop to listen. Anisa tilts her head. "Where's it coming from?" She looks around. "It might be in trouble—help me look for it."

Even now when she's the one hurt, Anisa's willing to

help an injured animal. That's one of the things I like about her but I can't let her do it. Not this time. "That's out. We have to go!" Guilt is starting to eat me up. "You might be getting a disease as we speak."

"Two more minutes won't hurt. Besides, I don't think it's bleeding so much anymore."

She's right. It has slowed down. If Anisa gets that disease, though, or something worse, I'll never be able to forgive myself. Best friends are supposed to help each other out of trouble not hurt. I hold up a finger. "One minute, then we're out of here."

As we get closer to the Porta-Potties, and I pinch my nose closed, I hear the cat again, only it's much louder. "I think it's coming from over there," Anisa says, pointing toward the Porta-Potties.

We follow the screeching, then stop in front of one of the Porta-Potties.

"Open the door so we can see," Anisa says.

"Not me. I'm still scarred from the last time I looked into one of these things."

"Okay, okay, move out of the way. I'll do it."

Anisa slowly opens the door.

"*Eeeowww, eeeowww.*" The noise is even louder than before. Each sound is quickly followed by another with barely a breath in between. The cat must really be sick.

Anisa pushes the door completely open, then freezes.

"What is it?" I ask.

"Oh, my God! It's a baby." Her voice goes up and down like a seesaw. "And it's all bloody."

"Yeah, right. Stop messing with me."

"I'm not." She moves out of the way so I can see.

On the floor, surrounded by dirty footprints and toilet paper, is a baby.

2

The baby's head seems too big for its body. Its red face is all squished up and its eyelids are fat and puffy. The hair is dark and pressed to its head in crazy directions. It's much smaller than any baby I've ever seen. I get a closer look to make sure it's not some kind of doll. Bluish-purple veins show right through its forehead and cheeks.

The baby is loosely wrapped in a white T-shirt, like the person who left it didn't want it touching the stuff on the floor. Seeing a baby alone in a place like this makes my legs weak and I say things that I know don't make sense.

"Maybe the mother forgot where she left it. Maybe she left it here for safekeeping. Maybe she doesn't know it's missing."

Anisa ignores me but I don't mind. I must sound brainless.

She goes inside while I hold the door open. I don't even notice the smell anymore. The baby lets out another scream.

"Is it okay?"

Anisa bends down beside the baby. Then, taking hold of

the shirt using only the tips of her fingers, she gently exposes the baby.

Thick white stuff covers the baby's body. Its tiny legs are kicking slowly at the air.

I can't understand what I'm seeing. Is there some kind of rope on its belly? The skin is so white and everything is so bloody—maybe the baby is hurt.

Anisa makes a weird sound like she's just lifted something heavy. "I think this baby was just born."

When I hear her words, my heart flutters around in my chest like it's not connected to anything anymore. I see junk like this on the news all the time but I never think too much about it. Maybe because it was on television, it didn't seem real.

Somebody leaving their baby all alone shouldn't be real.

"The umbilical cord is still attached," Anisa says.

I don't tell her I thought it was a rope.

Anisa's light skin turns red from her cheeks to her neck. That always happens when something upsets her or when she's worried. "We have to get her some help, Lionel."

I didn't even notice it was a "her." Maybe I'm in shock. That happens sometimes. My science teacher said so.

Anisa finally picks the baby up, leaving behind the bloody shirt used to cover her. She takes care of her three-year-old sister, Bella, all the time, so she looks like she knows what she's doing. I've never even held a baby.

The baby's face softens a little and her mouth starts to move like she's sucking on something.

"She's hungry. We have to get her some food. Let's get out of here," Anisa says.

My brain starts with its dumb panic stuff again. "We can't. What if her mother comes back looking for her?"

"She won't. She left her here because she doesn't want her."

I rub my stubbly head like it's a magic lamp. "You don't know that. If she finds out we took her baby, she could say we kidnapped it." Even as I say it, I know Anisa is right. The mother is never coming back here.

Anisa hugs the baby to her chest and starts to walk away. Wisps of her dark hair blow in the breeze. "It's okay, it's okay," she says over and over.

I follow. We pass two dump trucks and a mound of dirt. "Where are you taking her?"

"My mother will know what to do. We'll take her home."

The baby is crying again and I wonder if she's cold even though it's July. I take my shirt off and wrap it around her, but it doesn't stop her from letting out a good long wail. Carefully, I caress her head. Her hair is a little damp but softer and silkier than anything I've ever felt. "Sshhhh, baby. You're safe now."

Anisa smiles at me like I've done something more, and I get a warm feeling inside. "How's your leg?"

"It doesn't hurt anymore."

I'm not feeling guilty anymore either. Maybe we were meant to be here for the baby. Who knows if she would've survived until the workers showed up on Monday?

We forget all about the way we came in and head straight for the gate. Anisa and the baby go through the gate first. By the time I squeeze through, Anisa is already a few feet ahead, showing no sign of waiting for me. My feet may be big at size eleven, but they're going way too slow. I wish my Nikes could sprout some wings and take us home.

I notice Anisa's back to limping, but I can't let guilt take hold of me again. Not when I know we've probably just saved a baby from dying.

I catch up to her and we half walk and half run toward home. All the while, Anisa is talking to the baby. "We're going to get you some help. Don't worry, don't worry." But that doesn't stop her from crying. It's loud and high-pitched and sounds like she's in pain, like somebody is pinching her.

Some people stop and stare at us. Maybe they think we're doing the pinching.

An old woman wearing a straw hat the color of a peach and a suit to match asks, "Is everything all right?" I feel bad when we don't stop to answer, but we don't have a choice. Even though I'm not wearing a shirt, I'm sweating. My mother thinks it's disrespectful to walk around like this when you're not at the beach or the pool. She wouldn't be happy at all if she saw me.

A police car passes us, then puts the flashing lights on and makes a U-turn, which freaks me out.

When the car stops, both cops—one man and one woman—get out. The woman keeps her hands at her sides. Her fingers are long and spidery. Her face is plain and fresh like it was just scrubbed. She seems to be young, like she just got out of the police academy, and that might make her jumpy. I hope her hands don't nervously work their way up to her gun.

Not too long ago a young policeman in my neighborhood shot and killed a teenager. The policeman thought he was pulling out a gun when it was only a cell phone.

"Are you hurt?" the policeman asks, blocking our path. His name tag reads COSTELLO, and I'm almost as tall as he is. He's heavy and his face is red like he was running. His voice is stern, and even though he asked a question, it doesn't sound like one. At least not one where he actually cares about the answer. That makes me feel like we've done something wrong even though I know we didn't. I don't dare move. I don't want to make any trouble. I guess Anisa doesn't want to either, because her feet stay glued to the sidewalk and her face is as still as a stone.

"No," I say over the baby's cries.

Costello reminds me who's in charge. "I'm talking to your friend."

That makes Anisa flinch but makes me angry. We haven't

given him a reason to be nasty. I know to keep my mouth shut, though.

Stepping closer to Anisa, the policewoman asks, "Miss, is this your baby?"

Maybe she's lost her mind, because Anisa is just a kid.

"No." Anisa starts making a soft clicking sound into the baby's ear, then rocks from side to side trying to quiet her. "We found her."

The policewoman acts like she hasn't even heard what Anisa said. Instead she looks down at the blood on Anisa's leg. "Are you sure this isn't your baby?"

"I told you we found her." That's when Anisa tries to walk away, but Costello steps in front of her. "You can't keep me here! We have to go!"

The wind picks up a little and Anisa adjusts the shirt around the baby. Costello and the policewoman exchange glances, and then the policewoman asks Anisa again if the baby is hers.

Anisa starts to cry. "No! Somebody left her and we found her, right, Lionel?"

I have no idea why they don't believe Anisa but maybe they'll believe me. "She's telling the truth. We found her a few minutes ago." I don't say where. I don't want to get into trouble for being somewhere we weren't supposed to be.

The policewoman then says something to Costello about the baby being premature.

"She was born too early?" I ask. "Will she be okay?"

They don't answer my questions, so I start to ask again, but then Costello says something into his radio. The baby's crying makes it impossible to hear anything. Even though we did nothing wrong, I'm worried. If the baby is hurt and we didn't notice, they'll think we hurt her.

Five minutes later an ambulance rounds the corner with its siren blasting. Now it's the policewoman's turn to tell Anisa that everything is going to be okay. "My name is Maggie. What's yours, sweetheart?"

Anisa tightens her lips and refuses to respond. Tears furiously stream down her cheeks, and I have to look away or I might cry too. "We're here to help you, not hurt you," Maggie says, sounding a little more unfriendly.

The paramedics—two guys, one with a tiger tattoo peeking out from underneath his short sleeve and the other tall and skinny—get out and head for Anisa.

"Miss," the one with the tattoo says in a kind voice. He's a shorter version of The Rock. "Can you get into the ambulance by yourself or do you need our help?"

Anisa's words fly out now and we have no trouble hearing them over the baby. "No, I don't need your help or anybody's! Now, move out of my way and let me go!"

"You may be in shock," he says, putting his arm gently across her back. "It looks like you may have lost some blood and we need to get you to the hospital."

"I got a cut on my leg, that's all. It's not a big deal. I don't need to go to the hospital! I just want to take this baby home to my mother."

The baby is screaming like crazy and now her face is so red, it looks sunburned. Either she's getting hungrier or she doesn't like the sound of Anisa's yelling.

Costello shakes his head back and forth like he knows for a fact that Anisa is lying. "Miss," he says in a loud voice. "Either they take you or we take you."

"No! She's right." I have to tell where she got cut. I don't have a choice. My heart knocks around my chest like one of the pinball games at DeMarco's, the pizzeria where me and Anisa sometimes hang out. "She got hurt in the lot where they're building the new grocery store. That's where we found the baby. We're sorry. We'll never go back again, I swear."

People who want to know what happened crowd around. They're looking at us like we're aliens or something.

"I told you. It's just a cut and . . . ," Anisa says, looking down at the dried blood on her feet.

Costello doesn't listen to anything we say. The paramedics seem confused and look to him for directions. I hold my breath, hoping he'll let us go, but then he nods and puts on a pair of blue rubber gloves Maggie hands him.

Anisa shrieks, pulling the baby tighter. "No, stop!"

Even with Anisa twisting away from Costello, he's still able to take the baby from her.

The paramedics each take one of Anisa's arms to try

loading her into the ambulance but she doesn't go without a fight. She flails wildly, freeing herself and almost hitting the tattooed paramedic in the face. He grabs her tightly by the wrist. "Ouch! Get off of me!" she says.

"No, don't hurt her!" I say. "She didn't do anything!"

This is worse than any bad dream I've ever had. I just wish there was a chance I could wake up from it.

I bolt toward Anisa, but Maggie stops me. "Let me go!"

Maggie doesn't release me. Instead her grip tightens like a pair of pliers. Helpless and defeated, I say, "Anisa, don't worry! I'll go get your mother."

"No, don't leave me, Lionel!" she shouts, then kicks the tall skinny paramedic in the shin. "Don't make me go alone." Her lips tremble as she tries not to cry. "Please! I . . . I need you!"

The paramedic winces from Anisa's kick. "Please try to calm down. He can't come in the ambulance with you; it's against policy."

Anisa fights harder. Her hair breaks away from her ponytail and droops in front of her face. Her shirt twists and her skirt hangs lower than it should.

"But," the paramedic continues, "the police can take him. He'll meet us there, okay?"

I can't stand to see her like this, so I try my best to put her at ease. "He's right, Anisa, I'll meet you there. Please . . ." I don't know what to say. I look around at everyone and everything and I just can't believe it. "Please, Anisa, it'll be okay. You'll be okay."

"Let's go." Maggie points to the open door of the police car.

"I'll see you in a little while," I say one last time before collapsing into the car.

Anisa finally climbs into the ambulance.

The ambulance sirens pierce the air as we follow it. I never thought I'd be looking out the window of a police car and it makes me feel like a juvenile delinquent. A metal grate separates the front seat from the back. It smells sour, like they never open the windows. Sneaker prints cover the door and the seat back like some kind of dusty graffiti. They're even on the ceiling.

Maggie asks me for things like my name, my address, and my phone number. Then she asks for Anisa's information. She's busy writing everything down in a thick pad. When she's done, she asks Costello what he wants to eat for lunch.

While I listen to them talk about things that don't matter, I think of our mothers and how worried they must be. We were only supposed to go to the store for milk. My mom will go berserk when she finds out I'm in trouble with the police.

When we arrive at the hospital, the skinny paramedic rolls Anisa out of the ambulance on a stretcher. She's strapped down with thick orange belts. The tattooed paramedic carries the baby wrapped in a blue blanket. Now everybody will think it's a boy instead of a girl.

They wheel Anisa through the emergency room entrance first. Then Maggie opens my door and leads me into the waiting room.

The air conditioner must be on mega high because right away I'm shivering. I wonder what happened to my shirt.

The hospital is crowded. Some people sit on the floor because every chair is taken. All around them are grimy shoe prints coming from something that spilled and dried up a long time ago. Papers and tissues that people were too lazy to throw away litter the area by the door. A man in the corner is coughing, and a woman sitting near him is bleeding from her head. Her hair is knotty and wet. She's holding a rag to it while writing things down on a stack of paper.

Some kids are crying and some are running around like we're at a playground. Maggie sees a nurse she knows, so she stops to talk. I find out she's got one kid in fifth grade and an old dog that has to be put down. I guess she's older than I thought she was.

After Maggie's done, she leads me farther down the hall into a small windowless office where college diplomas and posters of smiling kids cover grasshopper-green walls. It's quieter here since we're away from the chaos of the waiting room. Maggie points to one of the two brown chairs facing a desk and tells me to have a seat. She stands close to the door.

I'm only sitting for a minute when a small lady with cool spiked white hair and a row of earrings in each ear walks in, carrying a folder filled with paper. Instead of regular sneakers or shoes, she's wearing white rubber Crocs that squeak against the tiled floor with each step. Her eyes are kind and the color of pennies. She smells sweet, like some type of flower, which relaxes me just a little. Hanging from her suit jacket is a name tag that reads J. LAM.

"So," she says with a big smile. "My name is Jasmina and I'm a social worker here at the hospital, but you, my friend, can call me Jazzy if you'd like."

She winks at me and I like her right away.

"Look at those goose bumps. Let's get you something to put on," she says, placing the folder on the desk.

She leaves the room and comes back with a hospital gown. "Sorry, this is all we have. Do you mind?"

I take it and put it on. Beggars can't be choosers. That's what Mom says when she doesn't give me exactly what I want.

The gown is thin and doesn't do much, but it's better than nothing. I wrap it as tight as it'll go.

Jasmina sits in the chair next to me. "So sorry for the tight quarters. My regular office, upstairs, is being renovated. So I've had to make do here. Now, what's your name, honey?"

Before I can answer, there's a loud knock on the door, and Maggie opens it. Costello strides in and stands as close to me as he can get. When I look at him I remember how mean he was, so I quickly turn away.

Jasmina lightly taps my bouncing knee. I didn't even realize I was doing it. "Thank you, officers, but I've got it from here."

"We'll be right outside this door," Costello says, like I'm a criminal he's expecting to break out. "Oh, and their mothers," he says, consulting a piece of paper, "Theresa Perez and Maria Torres, should be here any minute." I swear he sounds happy.

Maybe Jasmina hears it too. Her eyebrows go up, just like my teacher's when I tell her I don't have my homework. "That'll be just fine," she tells him.

"Don't be afraid," Jasmina says after Costello and Maggie leave. She pats my shoulder. "I'm going to help you. Everything will be okay."

But I don't know if I can believe her. It wasn't okay when Maggie said that to Anisa.

"Your name, sweetie?" she says.

"Lionel Perez."

"Hmmm . . . Lionel. That's not a name you hear every day."

She's not the first person ever to say that and I have to stop myself from copping an attitude with her.

I got my name thanks to Mom's weird obsession, Lionel Richie. Mom's parents were big fans and played his music constantly. I guess Mom didn't have a choice but to become a fan too. She'll listen to what's playing on the radio once in a while, but mostly Lionel streaming online is it.

I don't tell any of this to Jasmina, though.

"How old are you, Lionel?" she continues.

I concentrate on her earrings. Six in each ear. "Just turned thirteen."

"That makes your sign Cancer, the crab, like me. My birthday is two weeks away, July thirteenth. Seven one three, my lucky numbers!" She reaches for the folder she placed on the desk. "But I'm not telling you how old I am, so don't even think of asking." She smiles.

I laugh even though I don't really feel like it.

Jasmina puts her hand on mine. "Lionel, I know you're in a hospital and you must be scared, but I give you my word, your friend and the baby are safe here." She squeezes my hand a little and that makes me feel like she's on my side. I don't want her to let go, but she does. "And so are you. I just have to ask you some questions, okay?"

"Okay, but they said the baby might be premature. Does that mean she could . . ." I can't say the word, so Jasmina says it for me.

"Die?"

"Uh-huh."

"I don't know that, but I do know the doctors are taking excellent care of her."

That's not good enough for me. "But is there a chance?"

"Lionel, there's always that chance. Nothing is ever promised."

I sit straighter and clear my throat because I need to give

myself something to do other than sit here thinking about how the baby might not make it.

Jasmina takes a pair of zebra-striped glasses out of the pocket of her suit jacket and puts them on. Then she writes stuff down in the folder.

"Allrighty then. You told the police that you and Anisa found the baby, right?"

"Yes."

"Where did you find her?"

"In one of those Porta-Potti things." Thinking about how the baby looked in all that mess sneaks up on me and makes it harder to talk. I think about how she was left like she didn't matter, kind of like me.

I was seven years old when my father left. I've only seen him once since he left six years ago. He had come back for his winter coat and some tools he'd left behind.

Even though he stood in the cold hallway wearing nothing but a short-sleeved shirt and jeans, sweat glazed his face. He had lost some weight, too, in the three months he'd been gone. Where his shirt used to pull tight across his belly, it hung loose like a rain poncho.

I know he's alive because every now and then he'll send Mom a money order. The envelope hardly ever has the same return address on it. Last time it was somewhere in Georgia.

I swallow a few times before answering Jasmina's question. "She was on the floor wrapped in a white T-shirt, but we didn't take it with us."

"Hmmm . . . can you tell me where the Porta-Potti was?"

I tell her, but I hope she doesn't ask how we got in.

"Was there anybody else with you and Anisa?"

"No."

"Did Anisa leave you at any time while you were in the lot?"

I shake my head.

"Can you tell me how Anisa got hurt?"

"She fell on the edge of a steel beam and cut herself."

"Did you find the baby together or did Anisa find her first?"

"No, we found her together, but we thought it was a cat."

"A cat?" Jasmina says it like she's never heard the word "cat" before.

"Yeah, Anisa loves cats, so when we heard the noise, she thought maybe one needed help or something."

"Ah," she says, nodding. "I get you now. So what happened to your shirt?"

"I covered the baby with it so she wouldn't get cold."

She smiles and takes her glasses off. Her nose crinkles. "Are you and Anisa boyfriend and girlfriend?"

"No! My mom thinks that too, even though I tell her all the time we're not."

"What does your dad think?"

That's when something unexpected happens. Tears creep up on me and even though I quickly wipe them away, new ones emerge. It's like somebody pulled a plug. "My father . . . doesn't even know I'm alive."

My knee starts going again like it was wound up. I push the tears from my face with the bottom of the hospital gown. I'm so embarrassed.

"Oh, sweetie pie," Jasmina says. "I'm so sorry. Would you like to talk about it?"

Her voice is soft and comforting. It reminds me of how Mom used to wake me up in the morning when I was little. It was like Mom was trying to put me to sleep instead of waking me up. If I let Jasmina go on talking, I don't know what else I'll blurt out.

Just as I shake my head, Maggie knocks, then opens the door again. She hangs on to the knob with those crazy spider-fingers. "The parents are here."

Jasmina leads me into the hallway where Anisa's mother is standing with Costello, Maggie, and a doctor.

"No, *aqui*," Anisa's mother says, pointing to the floor. "Tell me here."

The doctor talks to her quietly. She's nodding her head a lot until she brings her hand to her mouth. The doctor pats her shoulder.

Maybe Anisa's in one of the rooms getting her leg fixed up or getting that shot she talked about, because I don't see her anywhere. Mom is just making it to the nurses' station when she sees me and Jasmina. I can tell she rushed to get here because she's still wearing her pajama pants, her worn-out bandanna, and her jacked-up '80s-looking glasses. They're so big, they almost cover her forehead. She never goes out in public like that.

"Lionel, what's going on? They wouldn't tell me over the phone. I was so worried. Were you crying? Are you okay?"

I fall into Mom's hug, feeling safe. My words are almost soundless against her shoulder. "I'm all right."

"Mrs. Perez?" Jasmina asks.

"Yes."

Jasmina introduces herself, then says, "Don't worry, Lionel is just fine."

"Why is he wearing a hospital gown?"

"Because," Jasmina says, holding her cold hand to my cheek, "he used his shirt to cover the baby."

Mom's voice is high. "Baby? What baby?"

Anisa's mother, along with everyone else in the hallway, looks over at us.

"I'll explain everything. May we talk in private?"

We follow Jasmina to her office but she stops me from going in. "I'm sorry, Lionel, I need to speak with your mother alone."

Mom gives me a long familiar look. It's the one she uses when she's thinking something bad but can't say what it is. Any relief I felt in her hug disappears.

3

At the nurses' station, I watch sick people as they're wheeled around in chairs or beds and I listen to the nurses complain about too much work.

Costello, Maggie, and the doctor lead Anisa's mother into the elevator. Her eyes meet mine just as the doors close. They're like two hard green marbles.

Mom used to be friends with Mrs. Torres, but when Anisa's father died of lung cancer, Mrs. Torres started acting like she didn't want to be bothered. No more phone calls or after-dinner coffee talk. When Mom confronted her about it, Mrs. Torres admitted that she thought it would be better for her to be friends only with people who were "saved." I know Mom was hurt but she was more mad than anything. Mrs. Torres even tried to break up my friendship with Anisa but stopped after I pretended to read the church pamphlets she gave me. I guess she thought she had a chance to "save" me too. So now when Mom and Mrs. Torres see each other, they only give a small pity hello. Mom once told me she pities Mrs. Torres because even though they're no longer friends, she knows she's suffering since losing her husband. I can only assume Mrs. Torres pities Mom because she believes Mom and I won't get into heaven without being saved. It's not like we don't believe in God, because we do. It's just that Mom doesn't believe God will lock us out of heaven just for not going to church. Mom says God's bigger than that. He doesn't care where your feet have been as long as your heart is in the right place.

In a way I'm lucky. When my father left us, all my mom did was pack up our stuff and move to a new apartment in a building across the courtyard. We still knew all the same people and everything, but she said she needed a place that didn't have his stink on it. At the time, I didn't know what it meant, but now I know it means she needed an apartment that didn't remind her of him or of how we used to be happy.

I can't stop myself from thinking about how the baby's going to feel when she finds out she wasn't wanted. That the people who were supposed to care about her the most didn't. Even though my father turned his back on me, at least I have my mom. I'll never do that to my kids. I'll be a better father, a better man, than he ever was.

I'm still thinking about my father when I spot Nelson, a puny kid with a big nose and braces. He lives in the building across from mine on the third floor. He's carrying a get-well balloon.

"What's up?" he asks, coming closer.

People call him Nosy Nelson. His bedroom window faces

the courtyard and you can see him peeking out from behind his curtain watching people like some kind of sorry Peeping Tom. He's the last person I'd tell anything to.

"Nothing."

"Are you sick or something?"

I almost say yes but I know that'll only make him ask two million questions instead of one million.

"No."

"Then what's with this gown?" He pulls on my sleeve.

I scan the hallway hoping to see Anisa.

"I said—"

"It's a long story, okay? What're you doing here anyway?"

"Me and my mom are supposed to be visiting my aunt but they took her for tests. I got bored watching Mom read a magazine, so I took a walk and ended up here."

"Well, there's nothing exciting going on here either," I say, noticing a big ketchup stain on the front of his button-down shirt. "You should just go back to your mother and leave me alone."

"What's up with the attitude?"

Mom's been with Jasmina a long time. It shouldn't take this long to tell her what happened. Unless they found out Anisa has that disease or maybe she has to have surgery on her leg. Or maybe Jasmina got a phone call telling her the baby died.

"What's wrong with you, Lionel? Lionel?"

He's like an annoying mosquito that just won't leave you

alone until he gets a taste of your blood. "Anisa got hurt, but she's fine. Everybody just overreacted, the end. See? Nothing exciting."

"Oh," Nelson says, looking at me funny.

"Why are you staring at me like that? You don't believe me?"

He runs his tongue across the wires in his mouth. "Why wouldn't I believe you?"

"Never mind," I sigh.

We don't say anything for a couple of seconds. Then Nelson starts tapping the balloon against the wall. "You sure Anisa's okay?" he asks, like he's disappointed he doesn't have something juicy to talk about.

"Yeah, I said she's fine, didn't I?"

I pace the floor, hoping Nelson will get a clue, but he doesn't.

"You know," he says, "I heard the police brought in a baby before. They said a thirteen-year-old girl had it outside in some dirty lot."

It takes me a second to realize what Nelson just said. I stop pacing and turn to him. "What did they mean when they said the girl 'had it'? Like, she was just carrying it? Like, had it in her arms?"

"No, dude. 'Had it' as in it's her baby. And speaking of having babies," he grins, "I mean, what's up with Anisa wearing those big shirts?"

Anisa and Eva started wearing their father's shirts after he died. Eva's are bigger since they're from a long time ago when their dad was heavy. I never told them I wear my father's shirt too. It's a T-shirt I found in a bag of rags Mom keeps around for when she cleans.

The shirts make Anisa and Eva look way bigger than they really are, but they don't care what people think. Anisa says all that matters is that they feel closer to their dad when they wear them.

"Was she trying to *hide* it?" Nelson continues. He puts his hand near his stomach and makes a rounded motion in the air.

Not saying a word, I take a deep breath, then make a fist. I get ready to throw a punch when both his hands shoot into the air. "Wait! Why're you being so serious? I'm only messing with you."

My heart is thumping hard. "Man, shut up. Just keep your big mouth closed for once in your life!"

I start pacing again. I don't even know where Anisa is. My stomach feels queasy like I'm seasick only I'm not on a boat. This whole thing is crazy. I just want this day to be over.

Nelson is only quiet for about thirty seconds. "I wonder where the father is. Does he even know he's got a kid? Maybe he's some loser who wouldn't care anyway."

The next thing I know, I'm charging Nelson. I've got him pinned against the wall. His balloon is free and heading toward the ceiling. Even though I have him by his bony shoulders and not his throat, his mouth tightens like he's holding his breath. His eyes bug out and fill with tears.

"GET OFF ME, MAN! WHAT'S WRONG WITH YOU?" he squeals.

But I can't make myself stop. I don't even want to. "I told you to shut up!"

An Asian nurse wearing lavender scrubs and a slicked-back ponytail rushes over and tries to pry my fingers open. "Stop! What's going on here? Security!"

Every eye is on me. Maybe they think I belong in the mental ward. One patient hides part of her face in her hospital gown like that'll protect her. People walk past practically hugging the walls so they won't have to come anywhere near me. *What am I doing?*

Finally, I loosen my grip. "I didn't mean it," I sputter. "Nelson! I'm sorry."

"Whatever! Just keep your hands off me!"

"Honey, are you okay?" the nurse asks him.

He wipes his sweaty forehead. "Yeah, I'm okay."

"I'll be at the desk if you need me, all right?"

The nurse gives Nelson back his balloon and gives me a death glare.

A tall, redheaded security guard jogs down the hallway a little late. His shiny black shoes pound the floor as his keys clank against his side. He has two big Hershey bars in his hand. I guess it was vending machine time. "What's the problem here?" he asks.

I don't have an answer for him but Nelson surprises me when he says that it's over and there is no trouble. If it was the other way around, I'd probably try to have his butt taken out in handcuffs.

The door to Jasmina's office finally opens and Mom marches out. She takes one look at the security guard hovering close to me and her face contorts like she just stubbed her toe. "Lionel?" She adjusts her glasses. "Is there something else I need to be worried about on top of this other business?"

"No."

The security guard seems satisfied and walks away.

"That's good," she snaps. "Because this baby stuff has already gotten you in more trouble than you want to be in."

Nelson takes a couple steps backward. "Baby stuff? Oh, man," he whispers from somewhere behind me. "I knew you were in some kind of trouble. Anisa too."

I should've punched him when I had the chance.

Mom focuses in on me like I'm the only one standing in the hallway. Each word falls out and stops short like it's a whole sentence by itself. "Get. Your. Behind. Into. Jasmina's. Office."

I follow her into the office. Nobody takes a seat, so I guess I'm expected to stand too. "Is the baby okay? Anisa?"

"Lionel," Jasmina starts, "Anisa's wound has been taken care of. You'll be glad to hear she didn't need any stitches and is doing well. She's being brought down as we speak so we can get this all straightened out. And we'll probably find out the baby's prognosis pretty soon too."

Mom stands against the wall with her arms crossed.

I just know Nelson must have his stupid ear up against the door listening to everything we're saying, but I don't care. "Mom, we didn't do anything wrong!"

"For your sake, I hope you didn't! If that baby is really Anisa's and you're the daddy—" She moves closer to me, never taking her eyes from mine. "Boy, you better run."

"Please, Mrs. Perez," Jasmina says, "calm down."

Mom ignores her. "I can't believe you'd go out and make a baby."

The baby, mine? My face is hot and it feels like all my blood rushed into my head and stayed there. I get this feeling a lot when I'm embarrassed, and having Mom think that me and Anisa did *it* is humiliating. "I didn't!" I yell. "We didn't!"

There's a knock on the door. When Jasmina opens it, Anisa and her mother walk in. Maggie and Costello are right behind them.

Anisa is wearing different clothes and her eyes are crazy swollen like she's been crying since forever. She won't even look at me.

"Mrs. Torres, please have a seat," Jasmina says to Anisa's mother.

She sits down without acknowledging anyone. Her lips are pursed, making her look like an angry fish. The hairs above her top lip are dark, even darker than what little I have going on above my lip.

Jasmina motions toward the other seat. "You too, sweetheart," she says to Anisa.

Anisa sits and that's when I see her leg is bandaged.

The office is cramped and stuffy and the only thing I can think of is breaking out. Costello is standing next to me, using his meaty arm to wipe beads of sweat from his forehead. Jasmina takes off her suit jacket and hangs it on a hook in the corner. Underneath each of her arms is a big wet spot. The door is only two feet from me. I close my eyes and try not to think about being on the other side of it.

"Anisa," Maggie starts, "can you tell us again what happened in the lot?"

Before she can answer, Anisa's mom butts in. Her Puerto Rican accent is thick. "It's been many months since he's been *en la casa de Dios. Siete!*" she says, waving her hand at me like I'm one of those annoying fruit gnats.

I stare blankly.

"Seven months since he's been in the house of God," she says. "Is too long!"

I stick my hands into my pants pocket so that I can move my fingers as I count in my head. That brings us to last Christmas, when me and Mom attended the candlelight service at the Catholic church where I was christened.

"That's ridiculous!" Mom says. "What exactly does all of this have to do with Lionel not going to church?"

"Everything! *Mi hija,* my daughter, is a good churchgoing girl and would never do something so terrible!" Her nostrils flare. "Maybe the real heathen," she continues, "the one who doesn't go to church, had one of his girlfriends put that poor baby in that disgusting place!"

Mom is off the wall in two seconds. Anisa's mother sees her coming and stands to meet her. Her lips are slightly apart now like she's about to growl or something. One eyebrow rises because she knows she's hit a nerve with Mom. They're so close to each other, I don't know how they can breathe.

I don't even know what a heathen is but it's definitely not a good thing. "Mami!" Anisa yells out.

"Maria, don't you ever," Mom starts in a low, dry voice, "talk about my son like that again. *Bruja.*"

It's true. With the way Anisa's mother is gritting her teeth, she does look like a witch.

Maggie puts her hand in between them to separate the two. "Let's remember that we're the adults here, okay?"

Without taking her eyes off the floor, Anisa quietly starts to repeat the story while pulling on the end of her ponytail. She doesn't get the chance to finish because the door opens and a tall doctor with thick messy hair enters, taking up whatever room is left. He seems too young to be any kind of doctor. "At Mrs. Torres's insistence, we've examined . . ." Anisa silently starts crying, but the doctor keeps talking. "Anisa and have found no evidence that she has given birth."

Mom sighs like she just ran a marathon.

Insistence? Examined how? Then it hits me. There could only be one way to check a woman to see if she's just had a baby. I can't believe Anisa's mother would make her do something so embarrassing. That's when I lose it. My mouth opens and I fill the room with words. "What is wrong with you? ALL of you. You had no right doing that! We RESCUED a baby. Why don't you get that?"

"Watch how you're talking, Lionel!" Mom says.

"No, it's not right!"

Before Mom can say something more, Jasmina reaches out for me, but I don't let her touch me. I don't want any of them touching me. "Calm down," she says.

The doctor gives Jasmina some paperwork before quietly slipping out the door.

"I'm leaving too!" I say, moving toward the door and bumping into Costello.

"I don't think so," he says, glancing at Mom.

"Yo, you can't hold me here. I didn't do nothing wrong! You can't keep innocent people against their will, and that's what I am. That's what WE are!"

"Maybe he can't, but I surely can," Mom says, pushing her glasses up on her nose. "And you'll leave when I tell you it's time to leave. What has gotten into you?"

Man, I'm raging. My heart is going stupid fast and I'm feeling strong enough to tackle even Costello.

"It's okay, Lionel," Anisa whispers.

"No! What they did to you ain't right! None of this makes any sense!" I throw a punch into the nearest wall. A big piece of green paint chips off, showing the white plaster underneath.

Everybody jumps. I surprised myself too and even though I hurt my knuckles, it felt good. Too good, because I want to do it again. I raise my fist but Maggie catches it before I make contact.

"Hey!" she says, digging her long fingers into my arm.

"Stop!" Mom screams, and I'm not sure if she's mad at what I did or scared of what the police might do to me.

Anisa's mother jumps from her chair and pulls Anisa out of the office with her. No one stops them.

My heart is still racing. "Does that mean we're done?" I ask.

"Yes," Jasmina says in a low voice, then hands Mom a card with her name on it. "In case you have any questions or concerns, please don't hesitate."

Costello and Maggie make their way through the door. Mom thanks them like they did us a favor or something. I want to ask her if she's crazy but I know she's past her boiling point, so I keep my mouth closed.

"Are you going to be okay, Lionel?" Jasmina asks, watching me pick at my polka-dotted hospital gown. I'm reminded of how much I liked her and her spiked hair, but now I'm not sure I like anybody.

I take a deep breath in order to calm down before answering. "Yeah, but what's going to happen to the baby? Is she okay?"

Jasmina's eyes are even kinder now than before. "Well, let's see," she says, flipping through the paperwork the doctor gave her. "So far, the baby is doing well, but we'll keep her here until we know for sure that she's completely healthy. Then we'll most likely have to find a foster home for her."

I know about foster homes. There was a boy in my class named Kevin who used to live in one. He told me he always had his bags packed because he never knew when he'd be sent to another foster home or he'd have to run away if the people were mean to him. Like one time, he lived with someone who used to hit him with an umbrella whenever he spoke without being spoken to first. They actually broke his eardrum once. It was a long time before he could hear out of that ear again. I even saw on the news once how a foster kid was kept in a cage and almost starved to death. I don't want to think about the baby living with crazy people like that.

After four months of sharing my snacks and hanging out with Kevin at lunchtime, he just disappeared. I never heard from him and for all I know he could've been killed.

Mom is shaking her head. She must be thinking about crazy people too. "No mother *and* no father? So sad," she says almost to herself.

"Fathers never care about nobody but themselves any-way," I say.

Mom shoots me a look that I know means to be quiet. "I'll be in the hallway," I say.

While I wait for Mom and Jasmina to say good-bye, the lady who was hiding behind her hospital gown earlier does an about-face when she sees me. Then she scurries off like a mouse.

I flex my fingers, thinking about how I punched the wall and made everybody pay attention to me. I'm not going to lie about it either—it felt good. Really good.

In the car, there is a bag of my old clothes. Whenever I outgrow something, Mom bags it up and drops it into a big metal box near the homeless shelter.

I reach into the bag and find an old shirt. Wearing a shirt one size too small is better than walking into the courtyard wearing a hospital gown.

Mom is quiet as she drives. I expected all kinds of yelling, but the silence is worse because I don't know if she's thinking about punishing me for something I didn't even do. We're getting closer to the construction site. Mom slows the car down, then pulls over. My stomach is knotting up.

There's a news van parked on the street and a police car in front of the fence. Behind it is a regular-looking Ford Explorer except it's all black with dark windows. Probably one of those sly undercover SUVs. If I was a police officer, I'd want to drive one of those.

A news reporter is talking to the few people who are hanging around.

Mom is slowly tapping the steering wheel while watching the crowd. I know she's doing some serious thinking. "We have a whole lot of talking to do when we get home," she says.

"Mom?"

She looks straight at me. I concentrate on the freckles across her nose. "Lionel, we need to have a baby-making talk."

I slide down in my seat, wanting to melt onto the floor.

"If your father was around, he'd be teaching you what you need to know. But . . ." She takes a deep breath and doesn't say anything else.

"But he's not, and I don't need him for anything anyway. I know all about that stuff, Mom."

"Seems you do but until you're married, I don't ever want to think about you becoming a father. I don't want my son going out there making babies all over the place like he's planting trees or something. You're not the Puerto Rican Johnny Appleseed."

"C'mon, Mom!" I turn to watch the crowd. I don't need the baby-making talk. We learned about that in school. It wasn't bad enough that we had to listen to Mr. Russo talk about how babies are made, but we also had to stare at a giant drawing of the entire male anatomy on the whiteboard in front of the room. Some of the guys made jokes about it but I wanted to hide my hot mortified face behind my textbook, but in Mr. Russo's class, if you did that, you might as well do the chicken dance because hiding brought just as much attention to you.

"Don't 'come on' me, nothing!" She gets out and slams the car door so hard everything shakes.

I roll down my window. "Where are you going?"

"Nowhere," she says, leaning on my side of the car. "I just need some air."

Why does she need air right here? "Mom . . ."

"Just give me a minute, okay?"

I know she's thinking about the baby. I am too and I'm full of questions I'll probably never get answered. Won't people ask where her mother is? How come she didn't love her baby enough to keep it? How come my father didn't love his enough?

"What kind of person leaves their child?" Mom says to herself.

She can't be for real. *The kind like my father,* I almost say. *That's what kind.*

The news reporter is packing up and people are starting to drift away from the fence. There was nothing to see in the first place.

Finally, Mom starts the car and we head home. She doesn't say a word and neither do I. After we've parked, I lag behind, giving us some space.

One thing you can bet on is if it's a hot day, nobody wants

to be inside. And since it's a Sunday plus the day after the Fourth of July, my courtyard looks like a big party.

Kenny and Johnjohn ride their bikes up and down a ramp made from plastic milk crates and a piece of wood. They both live across the courtyard from me. They say they're cousins but nobody believes them because Johnjohn is black and Kenny is white. I don't know why they can't just say they're best friends, but I'm not about to ask. They're troublemakers, and if one's not giving you a hard time about something, the other is. They're the kind of kids you always avoid, especially in the winter when they're throwing snowballs made of nothing but ice at everything that moves.

This one time I got lucky, though. While they were busy ambushing a group of kids passing through the courtyard, I was able to light up the back of Johnjohn's head with a big smooth snowball. I ducked behind a bench and laughed so hard I had to cover my mouth. The snow stuck to his wool hat in a perfect circle, looking like it was some kind of bull's-eye. I didn't stay behind the bench very long because Johnjohn was steaming mad, worse than I expected. It looked like that bull's-eye was about to melt right off his head. "Whoever did that," he yelled, "you're dead."

Then they took off in the wrong direction, giving me the chance to run for my life.

Today, Kenny's wearing Carmelo Anthony's number 7 Knicks jersey. Since Carmelo was born in Red Hook, he's like a hero around here. Not too long ago two kids argued over who was living in Carmelo's old apartment, like that counted for something. If Mr. Brown, the cool old guy from the building across from mine who's always wearing a Kangol Samuel L. Jackson-style, didn't break it up, they would've definitely started throwing punches.

Johnjohn pulls his bike into a skid, then nods in my direction. I nod back, then continue walking. I don't know what his deal is. He's never showed interest in being friends before.

"Man, didn't you learn anything from Mr. Russo's health class?" Kenny says as he rides past me. His floppy hair is stuck to his forehead like a wet paper towel.

His comment startles me and I miss the chance to say something back. Nelson's such a jerk. He must've cut his aunt's visit short just so he could get back here and talk trash. I catch up to Mom, who stopped to talk to Miss D. Miss D.'s real name is Dorothy. She used to babysit me and Anisa once in a while back when we were little.

The pink lenses of Miss D.'s eyeglasses give her cheeks a soft glow. It matches her voice, which she never raises. "Hello, Mr. Richie."

She calls me that because she knows how I got my name. I once confessed to her that I wished my grandparents were obsessed with a singer who has a cooler name. Not somebody from the olden days. Miss D. just laughed and said things could always be worse. Mom could've named me Cab, after Cab Calloway, some singer from the 1930s and '40s. Or something like Ludwig van Beethoven. That squashed my complaining right then and there.

"Lionel," somebody calls out. "Can you come here for a minute?" It's Royce, a kid from my building. He lives on the fourth floor and I live right below him on the third. Except for "hold the elevator," he's never said a word to me.

Mom keeps talking to Miss D. but takes a long look at Royce.

He's Puerto Rican like me, only he's a little darker and his mother doesn't make him keep his hair as short as mine. Royce is fourteen and goes to the George Academy, the school you can only get into if your average is ninety or higher. It's the same school Eva, Anisa's sister, goes to. She's a junior there.

It seems like Royce has everything going for him—good looks, brains, and lately, he's been wearing some nice clothes.

Today, Royce is sporting brand-new sneakers and a cell phone hanging from the front pocket of his jeans. He's standing with Little Tyke, a dark-skinned kid from a different project with an extra-wide forehead full of pimples. He's so short he looks like a third-grader, even though he's my age.

I remember my too-small shirt and try to stretch it out as I walk over to them. It doesn't work. I do my best to sound cool anyway. *"Wassup?"*

Tyke lowers his squeaky voice. "That's what we want to know."

"I guess you're talking about what happened with Anisa?"

"Yeah, what was smashing with her like?"

Music from the ice cream truck adds to the mix of bouncing balls and jump ropes hitting the ground. Four little girls run by screaming for the truck to stop. I have to move out of the way because one of them almost slams right into me.

"Man, don't talk about Anisa like that," I say.

Royce drapes his arm around me like we've been buddies our whole lives, and that makes me uncomfortable. "Okay, okay, just tell me how it was."

"There's nothing to tell," I say.

"Come on, Lionel—we already know anyway, we just want the details," Tyke says, trying to coax me. "Nelson almost broke his neck coming through here telling people . . ."

"Don't listen to Nelson, he's a liar," I say.

"But is it true or not? I vote for not, because I mean, you look like Sasquatch," Tyke says. "No girl wants to get with that."

Royce is trying not to laugh but he's not doing a very good job. A muted chuckle squeezes through.

I don't like feeling stupid and that's exactly how Tyke is making me feel. Mom scans the courtyard but lingers on us longer than I'd like her to. I'll have to keep my voice down even though I'm boiling inside. "Why are you concerned with the girls I might or might not be with, Tyke? You wishing you were me?"

Tyke busts out laughing. "Yeah, right. Nobody wants to be you. You probably don't even want to be you."

That almost sets me off, but with Mom so close I have to control myself.

"You know what? I bet Nelson left out the part about how I almost kicked his ass right there in the hospital." Now it's my turn to chuckle, only I don't try to hold it in. "And he's not the only one around here who needs to learn how to keep out of people's business."

A smile creeps up on Royce. "For real?" He sizes me up. "Yeah."

Mom calls me over and I walk away feeling good.

"Come hang with us later," Royce calls after me. "We'll be over by the basketball courts shooting some hoops."

I almost turn around to make sure he's talking to me, but I don't. Instead, I put a little hop in my step. I'm not sure why Royce wants me to chill with him all of a sudden. Maybe it's because now he sees I don't take junk from people. It didn't even matter what Tyke thought. "Yeah, I'll be there."

"Lionel," Mom says. "I told Miss Dorothy about what happened today and we were thinking it would probably be good for you if you had something to keep you occupied for the rest of the summer. And she's offered to give you piano lessons. Isn't that nice?"

I think Miss D. is the only one in our entire housing project who has a piano. It's not like a grand piano or anything, but it definitely still counts. When she used to babysit me, I'd sit beside her sometimes as she played. Her long brown fingers just flew across the keys. One note would lead to others and then an actual song—with her singing. Once in a while she'd try to get me to play something simple like "Jingle Bells" or even "Chopsticks." My fingers tripped all over themselves, but Miss D. only smiled throughout the whole confused mess.

Besides, I like to sleep until at least twelve in the summer. This definitely isn't *nice*.

I try hard not to let on how much of a dumb idea I think it is for me to try learning the piano again. Child prodigies are born, not made, so I'm pretty sure I missed that boat. "Thank you, but I don't really want to learn the piano," I say, watching nearby pigeons as they peck at sunflower seeds someone scattered on the sidewalk.

Mom puts her hand on the back of my neck and squeezes playfully. "Yes, you do. It'll be good for you. It'll keep you out of trouble too."

I don't get into trouble—I mean, not usually. I want to tell her that today really wasn't my fault, but I keep it to myself. She just might go into her baby-making talk right here in front of Miss D. "Okay."

Miss D.'s hands jump to life with a loud clap, scaring the pigeons and sending them into flight. Her peace sign earrings swing back and forth. "It'll be just like old times."

Mom adds more to this brilliant idea. "And besides, if you get bored learning the piano, I'm sure Miss D. could use your help around the house."

"Oh, Theresa, that won't be necessary." Miss D. blushes. "You know I have Mr. Owen helping me already."

Working doesn't make me happy either, but it'd be better than struggling with musical notes. "That's okay! I can help too."

"Well, Lionel, I don't know, but if it comes to that, I'll certainly pay you for any work you do."

"No need to pay him. His lessons will be enough payment," Mom says.

I've always liked Miss D., but I'd like her even more if Mom would let me work for real pay. I mean, Mom's job as a teller at Five Boroughs Savings Bank doesn't exactly let us starve but it definitely keeps me broke. My summer would be so much better if I had cash in my pocket. Instead it looks like I'll have nothing but "Mary Had a Little Lamb" running through my head. I nod to be polite. "When do I start?"

"Is tomorrow morning good?"

Mom answers for me. "That's fine. He'll be over at eleven."

As Miss D. walks with us to the building, Mom fills her in on how terrible Anisa's mom was acting. Miss D. *tsks* the whole way.

• • •

While I wait for Mom to bring up the promised baby-making talk, I think about Anisa and wonder if she'll have to suffer through a talk too.

After a few hours I begin to think maybe Mom changed her mind about the talk. But after dinner, when there's no rush to clean up and Mom stares at me from across the table, I know it's coming.

"Listen, I have no idea exactly what you know or what you think you know. But I'm telling you this: We're going to sit here until you understand the responsibility of being with a woman and the trouble you can get into if you're not ready."

I die inside and there's no textbook to save me from this sex talk. My ears burn with embarrassment. It's hard listening to your teacher talk about how babies are made, but it's way worse when it's your mother.

She pushes her plate away. "Do you know that when you have sex with one person, it's like you're also having sex with whomever else they slept with ever?"

Great, not only do I have to listen, but Mom expects me to answer questions too. This day can't get any worse.

I can't even look at her after she says the word "sex." That's a word you never want to hear coming from your mother's mouth. I stare at the salt and pepper shakers and wonder how many grains each bottle holds.

"Hmmm . . . Lionel? Did you?"

Gazing down at the leftover meat loaf on my plate, I feel nauseated.

"Are you listening?" She leans toward me, then repeats what she said, but it really makes no sense to me.

"How could that be if I only had sex—NOT that I did— with that one person?"

Things quickly roll downhill from there. She goes on and on explaining things I definitely don't want to know about, like diseases and girls and their menstruation.

When she suddenly stands and goes into the kitchen, I'm relieved. I stand too, but then she comes back and puts a banana on the table.

"Sit down, we're not done," she says, taking a condom out of her jeans pocket.

The sight of the condom almost kills me on the spot. As a matter of fact I think my heart stops beating for a few seconds.

"Mom, no!" I shriek, ready to escape into the safety of my bedroom. "You don't have to. Mr. Russo already did!"

"Lionel, that's all well and good," Mom says, tearing open the condom packet. "But I just need to make absolutely sure you know how to put this on."

Mom begins unrolling the condom onto the banana. I'm pretty sure I'll never be able to eat another one ever again.

"This is what it should look like," Mom says, holding the banana toward me.

I cover my eyes and groan.

"Lionel, please look at me."

I peek through my fingers.

"Okay," Mom continues, still holding the banana. "It's important to remember that you are never to use the same condom twice."

"Mom . . . !"

Mom takes off her glasses, then rubs where the nose piece left indents. I think this torture might finally be over, but after a minute she says, "I'm sorry but you need to know these things."

Mom takes a seat across from me. "I never told you this, Lionel, but when I got pregnant with you, your father and I weren't married. We were just teenagers—I was seventeen and your father was eighteen. I was terrified and didn't know what I should do. At first I was in denial. Kept telling myself that I was gaining weight because I was overeating or that I miscounted the days of my last period. The thing that absolutely scared me the most was what my mother would do to me."

I knew my parents were young when they had me, but it's weird to know just how young.

"Why're you telling me this now?" I ask.

"Because." She takes my hand in hers. "I think it's important for you to know that your father was pressured into marrying me by my parents, and you see how that worked out, right?"

Loud fire trucks race past our building. I'm thankful for their noise because Mom stops talking as they go by. "We did things backward and paid for it," she continues. "I don't want that happening to you. I love you too much to stand by and watch you let your future slip away without living up to your potential . . ." Her voice grows softer and harder to hear. "Without fulfilling your dreams."

Mom takes hold of both my hands and kisses them. I wonder what her dreams were, but I'm too afraid to ask. She gave them up for me and that's something I don't want to think about.

When Mom's eyes fill with tears, I realize this day has been too much for both of us and now everything feels heavy.

"I wasn't sure if this was what I wanted in my life," Mom says.

This? "You mean me? You didn't want me?"

"Oh, baby, that's not what I'm saying," she says. "It's just that I wasn't sure I wanted to be a mom. But everything changed the minute you were born. It only took one look at you to know I had done the right thing."

It blows me away thinking how easy it could've been for Mom to make the same decision the baby's mother made. If she had, I wonder what kind of life I would be living now. I mean, in five years I'll be eighteen and in college. I'm not sure I'd have that kind of chance if I'd been left. I might've even died.

I look to the ceiling hoping my own tears will go back to where they came from, but it doesn't work like that and they fall one after the other.

Mom pulls me close. I didn't know just how much I needed her to do that, and I snuggle in like I'm five years old. We stay this way for a long time, and when it's over, I'm so exhausted I can barely stay awake. Mom excuses me from helping to clean up. I lie in bed wondering how Anisa is doing. Even though her mom isn't the crying type, I hope Anisa's getting love too.

Tomorrow has got to be better than today, even if I am banging on Miss D.'s piano like a little kid.

As tired as I am, sleep doesn't come right away, and I start thinking of my father and what he'd say about everything that's happened. Maybe he would've known right away that we're heroes. I wonder if he'd be proud of me.

The next morning, Latin music curls itself into my sleeping ears. Congas, bongos, trumpets, and saxophones force me awake. Mom must've set my alarm clock before she left for work. I keep my eyes closed and feel around my night table for the off button, but I can't find the clock. Even with the pillow over my head I can still hear the congas' thumping beat. Just when I think it's over, a trumpet blasts and that's when I hop out of bed.

The bright red numbers on the alarm clock tell me it's only 10:00 a.m. I hit the off button and climb back into bed for fifteen more minutes, but I can't fall asleep because the courtyard is too noisy already.

Someone is whistling loudly—two high-pitched tones, the kind you have to put two fingers into your mouth to get. A little kid fake-cries directly outside my window.

"Wahhhh, wahhhh!"

"Don't worry, baby, I'll rescue you!" a girl happily announces.

I slam the window shut. There's no doubt that they're playacting for my benefit. People should be treating me like a hero, and I should feel like one too. But all the drama at the hospital just stole that away from me.

It's only been one day but I wonder if they found out who the baby's mother is yet and whether she's worried or even sorry. Maybe she's relieved that she can just go on with her life like she doesn't have a kid, the way my father did.

I wonder what he says when people ask him if he has any kids. Maybe he lies and says he doesn't, or maybe he tells them I'm dead. Maybe he believes having a kid who died is better than having a kid you abandoned.

But I can't waste my time thinking about my father all day because number one, I know he's not thinking about me, and two, I have to go up to Miss D. and check on Anisa to make sure she's okay. Yesterday was way harder on her than it was on me, even with Mom's sex talk.

After a quick breakfast, I throw on a T-shirt that actually fits me and the same pants I wore yesterday. I realize

I never bought the milk yesterday. A big five dollars. I hope she doesn't ask for it back.

First I go down one flight to Anisa's second-floor apartment and knock on her door. There's no answer, so I take the elevator up to Miss D.'s. I'll try again later.

When the elevator doors open, Mr. Owen, Miss D.'s neighbor, is locking his door. He's wearing a Mets baseball cap covering most of his gray hair, a collared shirt, a pair of checkered shorts, and his signature Nikes. His beard is patchy, with tiny white hairs popping out of his dark brown skin. Mom calls skin like his "silk chocolate."

"Hello, Lionel. What brings you way up here?"

"Miss D. wants to give me piano lessons."

"Well, now. That's mighty fine. So why are you wearing a frown the size of Manhattan?"

"Because I'd rather just do chores for her."

Mr. Owen slips his keys into his pocket. "That's very admirable, Lionel. It seems like young boys would rather be hanging out and running around like the world revolves around them instead of helping out their *community* like we did when I was a boy."

He stretches out each syllable in "community" like it's the most important word in the world.

"But," he continues, not taking his eyes off mine, "learning a musical instrument will make you smarter . . . it'll be just like learning another language."

If I'm going to learn another language it should be

Spanish. Now, that'll be useful. Even though Mom is full-blooded Puerto Rican, she never taught me how to speak it. I wish she had. At least I'd be able to understand what Anisa's mother says about me. Even my father, who is black and grew up speaking only English, knows more Spanish than I do.

Mr. Owen grins big and starts down the steps. "A very smart man once said, 'Most of us go to our graves with our music still inside us, unplayed.' Don't let that happen to you, Lionel."

I want to ask him what that means exactly, but he's already on the floor below, though still talking. "Have a nice time now. Miss Dorothy is a heck of a woman."

It doesn't take Miss D. long to answer the door after I knock. Makes me wonder if she was standing there waiting for me. "Good morning, my little chickadee," she croons.

She's wearing red lipstick and a long pink flowy skirt. Miss D. makes a lot of her own clothes on a sewing machine she keeps in her extra bedroom. I wonder if she made what she's wearing today.

A silver butterfly hanging around her neck from a piece of brown leather reminds me of Eva. She loves anything that has to do with butterflies. She even has a backpack shaped like one. Not much fits inside and she has to carry her fattest textbooks in her arms but it doesn't seem to bother her.

Miss D. interrupts my thoughts. "Are you ready for your first lesson?"

"Not really. I'm more ready to do some work for you, though. What do you have for me? Want me to take the garbage out? Sweep your floors?"

"My, my, Lionel. The piano isn't a torture device! If you really want to help that bad, I'll find you something to do after your lesson. Deal?"

Sounds like a deal all right. One where I lose. I nod and drag myself through the door.

5

Inside, the air is cool like in the library, and that kind of makes me feel a little better. We just have fans in our windows. Running air conditioners is too expensive.

In the living room, there's a big television facing the couch and one of those chairs that recline all the way back. The chair is exactly the kind my mother's saving up for. The piano sits in the corner next to a bookshelf. After falling in her apartment last Halloween, Miss D. had a nice blue wall-to-wall carpet installed. It runs from the living room to the back where her bedroom is.

It was a month after Anisa's father died, and I couldn't believe the bad luck that was making the rounds in our building. It had me a little worried too. My best friend's dad and Miss D.? Made me wonder what would happen next.

Mr. Owen said when he realized she wasn't handing out candy to the kids, he knew something was wrong. They had just gone shopping the day before and bought three bags of mini chocolate bars.

When Mr. Owen knocked on Miss D.'s locked door, she

yelled out for help. While Mr. Owen called 911 I talked to her through the door and told her everything was going to be okay.

Miss D. had tripped on a broken floor tile and couldn't get up. It seems like the floors in the projects are harder than anyplace else. Mom says they're made from concrete, the same as the sidewalk outside. Miss D. broke some ribs and her wrist. It was terrible to see her in so much pain and I wished there was something I could've done to help her. When she saw me she reached for my hand. I held on for as long as the EMTs let me, and then Mr. Owen took over and got into the ambulance with her.

After Miss D.'s fall, Mom was mad. She said old people shouldn't be allowed to live by themselves and that Miss D.'s son Matthew and his wife should be ashamed for not taking better care of his seventy-year-old mother. I think so too. I can't imagine not being there for my mom if she needed me.

When Miss D. came home from the hospital, Mom checked in on her for a month straight, before and after work. We'd eat in her apartment, and whatever we'd have for dinner, she'd have too, even though sometimes it was just fast food. I thought Miss D. would hate eating burgers and french fries, but it seemed as though she liked it as much as I did. She was funny about it too. Sometimes she'd make me look away at something, then steal one or two of my fries. After she got better, she insisted on taking care of herself, no matter what Mom said to try to change her mind.

In front of Miss D.'s living room window sit two plants almost as big as me. Their shiny leaves are long and skinny with pointy tips. Two smaller plants hang from the ceiling above and are bursting with yellow flowers the size of ping-pong balls.

I ignore the piano's gleaming white keys and the red-and-white-striped bench in front of it. I plop down on the couch instead, sinking deep into the cushions. I'm sure I could fall back to sleep here.

I wonder where Anisa could be and hope she's okay. I think about what her mother made her do in order to prove the baby wasn't hers and I get a sick feeling in my stomach.

Just then Miss D. holds her hand out to me. "Up you go. Can't hit those keys from there, now can you?"

Reluctantly, I take her hand, and we make our way to the walnut-colored piano.

The wood is super shiny and smells like lemons. Miss D.'s butterfly necklace reflects back at us, but everything else is just smudges of what we actually look like.

"You're awfully quiet this morning," she says playfully as we sit side by side on the bench. "Cat got your tongue?"

"Oh, I, um, I don't have anything to say."

"Is that right?"

I shrug my shoulders.

"Well, when you were little, you talked like somebody wound you up. But after everything that happened yesterday, I can understand," Miss D. says.

She taps her temple where little silver hairs curl. Mom calls them baby hairs, but I don't know if a person as old as Miss D. could have baby anything. "Listening gives your brain time to think."

I look at the empty spot where the sheet music usually sits. "Where's the music?"

"I'm going to try something new with you, Lionel. We're going to go all the way back to the beginning." She reaches onto the nearby shelf and retrieves two wooden sticks.

I'm really confused. I thought she was going to teach me the piano, not the drums.

That gets me thinking how cool it'd be if Miss D. did play drums instead of piano.

"I thought I'd start with teaching you rhythm. Now"—she hands the sticks to me—"bang four times."

"You want me to bang on your piano?"

"Yes, but *lightly.*"

I gently tap the wood above the keys. One, two, three, four. "Now what?"

"Okay, good. I want you to harness the sound, Lionel. Tap four more times, but don't play on three. So it's like this: *tap, tap,* hold, *tap.*"

She has me do that over and over, changing up the "hold" part so that the tune is different every time. It's kind of fun too.

"See how the rhythm keeps going even after you pause?"

I nod.

Then Miss D. tells me about middle C, and how it's the starting point for many songs. She also teaches me the B note and reminds me not to ball my hands into fists by telling me to imagine that I've got a tennis ball in the palm of my hand. That part makes me feel like a little kid because I should be able to keep my hands in the right position without pretending. But even with that the lesson isn't as bad as I thought it would be.

After forty-five minutes, Miss D. ends the lesson by telling me she doesn't want to wear me out on the first day. Then she plays a song, something so fast and upbeat that even I have trouble sitting still. I clap my hands in rhythm as I watch hers dance across the keys. When she's done, she stands and curtsies, which makes me laugh.

"So," Miss D. says, making her way toward the kitchen. "Would you mind going to the post office to buy a stamp and mail something for—"

Finally! I'm on my feet and stretching out my legs before she finishes her sentence. Hopefully Anisa is home now. "Sure."

"Good, good. And when you get back, how about cleaning the windows for me? Mr. Owen isn't a fan of washing windows."

Neither am I, but I agree anyway. "Okay."

"I'm so happy you'll be up here with me, Lionel!" She squeezes my cheek.

Even though I like Miss D. a lot and being with her isn't bad, I don't want to take lessons every single day. This is supposed to be summer vacation, not peewee music camp. Mom wants me with Miss D. because she thinks it'll keep me out of trouble, but I don't think that's fair at all. It's like I'm being babysat and I'm too old for that.

Last summer I was free to do whatever I wanted. Usually I slept late, then got Anisa and did all kinds of things, like playing in the park, hanging out at the library, or just sitting on the bench outside our building talking. Sometimes, if Eva went with us, we were allowed to go to the Red Hook pool. That's how summer is supposed to be. But so far I've only gotten to sleep late a couple of times and sit on the bench with Anisa. I was hoping Mom would let me go to the pool alone now that I'm thirteen but that probably won't happen. I don't regret finding the baby. It's just that I miss my freedom.

I stuff the envelope into my back pocket, then race down the steps to Anisa's apartment.

I knock on Anisa's door, then turn away so that I don't have to look at the peephole. People always look like *bombilla* heads through them. That's one of the few Spanish words I know and it means "lightbulb." Since my head is already enormous and hairless after my summer cut, I might look like the King of the *Bombilla* People through a peephole.

After I knock two more times, Anisa finally opens the door. Her mother stands behind her, wearing a flowered button-down apron that looks more like a shirt than something you wear only to get crusty and gunked up with food. And a red paisley bandanna, like the kind a cowboy wears around his neck, is tied tightly on her head.

The smell of my favorite meal, *pollo guisado*, chicken stew, drifts out and suddenly I'm starving.

On the weekends when my father was around, we'd all be up and dressed and ready to go on a bike ride, or maybe if the weather was really good, to Coney Island. Then when we'd get home, Mom would cook what my father called a tasty feast. Sometimes it'd be *pollo guisado* but sometimes we'd be lucky enough to have *pasteles*. That's a Puerto Rican dish made with green plantains, taro root, potatoes, pork, and spices. Some people put green olives in them and that's how I like them best. They come wrapped in a banana leaf and tied with string, like a gift. Since my father left, dinner has been kind of boring. I can't even remember the last time I had *pollo guisado*.

Anisa's eyes and nose are red. She's wearing a scarf on her head and one of her mother's aprons. Bella is holding on to her legs.

"Hi," I say. It sounds more like a question.

"Go away," Anisa says.

"What? Why?"

"Bad boy," Bella says.

Anisa's mother shoves Anisa from behind. "Tell him."

"I'm not allowed to be friends with you anymore."

"Tell him what I said," Mrs. Torres says. Her green eyes flicker with hate. "All of it."

Anisa looks to the ceiling and a couple of tears escape. "I can't be friends with you anymore because you're a bad influence on me."

Her words cut into me. It seems like I've always had Anisa and I can't stand the thought of being separated from her.

"You can't be serious," I whisper to the green-eyed devil, even though I'm watching Anisa.

Her mother starts closing the door. But I use my arm to hold it open. Feeling desperate, I plead my case. "It's not fair. We're being punished for doing something good."

Eva, still in her nightgown, comes to my defense. "Mami," she says, standing beside her mother. "Lionel's right. He hasn't done anything wrong."

Mrs. Torres moves Eva out of the way, then says, "Life's *no* fair." A vein running from her hairline to her dark eyebrows looks swollen. "Better get used to it now."

Eva and I lock eyes; then she shakes her head slightly and looks to the floor. I think she's embarrassed. I guess we both know she's not going to change her mind. I'm happy she tried, though.

When Anisa's mother is done with me, she turns her attention to Anisa. "*Mi hija,* yesterday was only a warning, a sign of what could happen. I want you to stay away from that boy, understand?" She says it like I'm invisible, then roughly grabs Anisa's arm. "Do you understand me?"

"I do, Mami!"

Everything inside me just stops.

The last thing I see before I take off down the steps is Anisa's face buried in her hands.

The feeling I had with Nelson at the hospital works its way up my back and into my head. It's prickly and hot. On my way out of the building I kick the door to the elevator as hard as I can.

A baby is alive because of us, I tell myself over and over. *We're heroes and nothing else.* If only everyone else saw it that way.

I'm still heated when I get outside. Royce and Little Tyke are sitting on a bench goofing around. Two benches down, Mr. Owen is playing cards at a folding table with Mr. Brown and Mr. Santiago. They're a pretty tight group and play cards a lot. Sometimes dominoes.

There's a cooler on the ground next to them. It's probably filled with snacks and drinks. I guess they plan to be out here all day.

Mr. Brown is the tallest and skinniest of the bunch. Today he's wearing shorts, yellow socks, and a yellow Kangol to match. Mr. Brown's wife had a stroke a couple of years ago and lives in a nursing home in Carroll Gardens. He says she'll be out soon but I'm not sure about that. I heard she's really bad. He visits her first thing every morning, then again around dinnertime. Sometimes when you see him coming back he looks all broken-down. Kind of hunched over and walking so slow you'd think he was lost. You can't help feeling bad for him.

Mr. Santiago is older than Mr. Brown and Mr. Owen. His wife died before he moved here from the Bronx a long time ago. It seems like he needs somebody looking after him too, because most of the time his pants have stains and stuff on them. Sometimes his memory slips and he thinks he's still in the navy. I've even seen him saluting people. If he's not hanging out with Mr. Brown or Mr. Owen, Mr. Santiago is usually at the library or fishing down at the end of Columbia Street if the weather is good. I never see him carrying back any fish, though, and that's good because anything you catch in the Gowanus Bay can't be healthy. You might wind up glowing in the dark or something.

It's weird because even though Mr. Owen lives in my building, I don't know all that much about him, except that his wife died before I was even born.

Mr. Brown stretches out his long legs. "Come on, Big S, show me what you got."

"Booyah," Mr. Santiago says, slamming down his cards.

"I guess he showed you," Mr. Owen teases. "And what exactly do you know about some 'booyah'? You're even older than we are."

"Don't you worry about what I know."

They're all laughing when Mr. Owen catches sight of me and calls me over.

"What's with the clenched fists? You ready for a fight or something?"

I shake out my sweaty hands. I don't know how long I've had them balled up, but it feels like it's been hours and now they're stiff. "No, I'm good."

Mr. Owen eyes me suspiciously. "Thought you were busy with Miss Dorothy and your piano lessons."

"Hmmm," Mr. Santiago mumbles underneath his breath. "You spend a lot of time up there, William. She teaching you piano too? Must be a bona fide concert pianist by now."

At first Mr. Brown holds in his laughter, but then he starts to crack.

"I was," I say finally. I wave the envelope at him. "Now I'm on my way to the post office for her."

"Is there something wrong, young man?" Mr. Owen asks.

"No," I say.

"Obviously there's something wrong," Mr. Brown says, exchanging glances with Mr. Santiago. "So why don't you just tell us what the problem is. People don't walk around with clenched fists for nothing."

I have to loosen my free hand for a second time.

"Yeah, there's nothing we can't help you figure out or fix. Together, we're over two hundred years old," Mr. Santiago says. "That's a whole lot of life experience we'll be able to lay on you."

"Two hundred?" Mr. Brown says in alarm, as if Mr.

Santiago just announced he eats dogs or something. "Don't tell the boy that. He might go thinking our brains have turned to sawdust by now."

The only one not laughing is Mr. Owen. He's busy smoothing over his beard, looking all serious. For the first time I notice that his ears poke out a little more than they should. I don't know why he's looking at me so hard. He hasn't taken his eyes off me once.

"Lionel," Mr. Brown says. "Don't pay this old fool any attention. Tell us what's on your mind."

Having all eyes on me is awkward. Compared to some of their problems, mine would probably seem like nothing to them. I'm just about to make up something lame when Royce calls me over. "Yo, we might go get something to eat. You want to hang with us? My treat."

Funny how just a few days ago I would've never thought Royce would be the one to save me from anything, and here he is rescuing me from this conversation. "Nothing. Everything's cool with me, Mr. Brown. I gotta go."

"Hold on a minute now," Mr. Santiago says. "Miss D. told Mr. Owen about the baby you rescued yesterday. How's she doing?"

They're all waiting for my answer and I feel like an idiot for not having one for them. I make up my mind to find out, though. "I'm not sure, but I'm going over there in a little while."

"Well, we're hoping she'll be just fine."

"Me too." I hurry over to Royce.

"Can't now, I'm busy," I say to him.

"Busy doing what?" Tyke picks at the constellation of pimples on his forehead.

If he saw me with those wooden sticks, he'd have a whole lot to say. "Just some stuff."

Royce checks his cell, then says, "No big deal. Find us when you're done, that's all."

"Yeah," Tyke says, rubbing his hands together. "Then you can tell us what really happened between you and Anisa."

Mr. Owen and his friends quiet down immediately. When I see him watching, I smile so he knows I see him grilling me, but it doesn't stop him.

Royce notices Mr. Owen too. He shoves Tyke, then whispers, "Quiet."

"I already told you Nelson is a liar, so stop bringing it up, Tyke. Anisa ain't even like that anyway."

Royce holds his fist out to me and I pound it. "You cool for sticking up for your friend like that."

Tyke just glares. He must not like Royce thinking anyone but him can be cool. Mr. Owen and the guys go back to their card game and I leave the courtyard and head to the post office.

After waiting in line to buy a stamp, I mail Miss D.'s envelope, then walk toward the hospital.

I think about Anisa on the way. I know her mother

made her say those messed-up things but I'm confused. She could've made some eye contact with me, kind of like a signal or something—anything to let me know she didn't really mean what she was saying.

My watch says it's almost one o'clock. In another hour and a half, Anisa will be on her way to Bible camp. I'll catch up with her after the hospital and see what she has to say.

I make it to the hospital pretty quickly and go straight to the main entrance. Luckily, it's visiting hours and no one stops me.

The door to Jasmina's office is open. She's standing at a filing cabinet, reading something in a folder. Today she's wearing pink Crocs with purple socks peeking out. They match a sweater hanging off the back of the chair I sat in. The hole I punched in the wall looks bigger today.

I knock lightly on the door frame.

"Lionel," she says, turning toward me. "What a nice surprise."

"I'm sorry for interrupting you."

Her Crocs squeak against the floor like it's wet. "Eh, don't worry about it, I could use a break." She touches my arm. "Come on in and have a seat."

She takes off her zebra-striped glasses. "How're you doing?"

"I'm okay, but I've been thinking about the baby. Is she still here?"

"Oh, honey, that's so sweet of you. Yes, she's still here. She'll remain in our custody for a little while." Jasmina is so pleased with what she has to say next, her face lights up. "And not only do we already have a foster family lined up for her, but they've expressed interest in permanently adopting her. That is, of course, if a family member doesn't claim her. Isn't that just terrific?"

My stomach feels heavy, like there's a bowling ball in there. "When are they taking her?"

"The paperwork is moving along quite nicely, so I'd say most likely Friday."

I sit up. It doesn't make sense. Today's Monday. "That quick? I thought she was premature."

"No, just a bit underweight, but she's eating so well that she'll gain in no time. Would you like to see her?"

I'm on my feet before I speak. "Yes."

In the hallway we pass the nurse who stopped me from beating up Nelson. "Everything okay, Jasmina?"

"Just peachy, Lucille. On our way to visit little Baby Doe. This is the young man who helped rescue her."

"Oh, I know exactly who he is." She says it like my face is on a wanted poster somewhere. I study Jasmina's rubber shoes.

We take the elevator to the third floor, then walk through a door that reads HOSPITAL EMPLOYEES ONLY. The room is more like a large closet. One chair, a sink, a tall garbage can, and shelves piled high with the same polka-dotted hospital gown I wore yesterday and some towels.

Jasmina has me wash my hands, then put a gown on over my clothes. Then, after putting on her own gown, she unlocks another door by punching some numbers into a small wall panel.

This next room is the nursery and it's much bigger. Six large windows look out into the hallway so that visitors can see the babies.

There's seven babies in all and some of them seem huge, with big round heads and chubby cheeks, while others are scrawny, with pointed heads and longish hair.

I ask Jasmina about the tiny white pimples on some of the babies' faces.

"Oh, those bumps are caused by blocked oil glands. They'll disappear soon."

Each little crib is more like a clear plastic box the size of a laundry basket. They're on wheels and have information written on large index cards attached to the front of the crib. Stuff like last name, male or female, and date of birth. Off to the side are two wooden rocking chairs, each with Winnie-the-Pooh characters painted brightly on the backs.

Two people, a new mom to one of the babies dressed in pajamas and an older man using a cane, look in through one of the windows to ooh and ahh over one of the babies. The older man keeps wiping his eyes with a tissue but his smile stays in place the whole time. I want somebody to look at the baby we rescued that way. With so much love for her that it bubbles up and overflows.

"Here's the little princess." Jasmina leads me to a crib that reads BABY DOE and the date we found her. "Isn't she just beautiful?"

She's in her own category when it comes to looks. Her head is a normal size and her face is perfectly round and clear. She's like a small pink rosebud—beautiful and smooth. Her dark silky hair is brushed into what looks like a tiny mohawk. She's the prettiest baby in here. The only thing she has in common with the other babies is that she's wrapped tightly in a green-and-yellow blanket. I smile, thinking how much she looks like a little burrito. She isn't crying now but sucking happily on a pacifier. I'm glad because I think she's cried too much already. I force myself not to think about how somebody threw her away. "She's . . ." I'm surprised by my need to catch my breath. It's another second or two before I can finish. "Perfect."

As soon as I say it, I know the word "perfect" isn't good enough. It's even more than that, but I'm having trouble putting my feelings into something I can understand. All I know is I want this baby never to be hurt or left ever again.

We watch her quietly as she stares off somewhere and I wonder what she's thinking about. When I lean into the crib to get a better look, her hazel eyes find mine. She doesn't blink or turn away and it's almost like she knows me. I finally realize that the feeling I have is love. But not the kind of love I have for my mom. It's scary and good at the same time.

"Can I hold her?"

"I think I can arrange that," Jasmina says. "Have a seat in one of the rocking chairs and I'll find a nurse."

The nurse introduces herself as Cheryl. She's short and wide and wearing purple scrubs decorated with baby bunnies. A bright orange headband holds her red hair away from her face. It's the kind of red that looks more like red velvet cake than the kind you're born with. Her eyebrows are bushy and red too. She's nice, though, much nicer than Lucille. I wonder if that would change if she knew how I acted yesterday.

After instructing me on how to hold a baby, Cheryl places her in my arms and right away it feels like everyone else has vanished and it's just me and her. She's small and delicate and as I watch her fall asleep, I hold her closer and feel my love for her growing into something powerful and new. I look at the man and woman still at the window and that's when it hits me that my love is bubbling up and overflowing too.

"All right, Lionel." Cheryl laughs energetically. "You seem to be a natural at this. Would you like to feed her?"

"I don't know. What if she chokes or something?"

"Don't worry about that, sugar, you won't be alone. I'll be close by. I'll be right back with her bottle."

"She's doing quite well." Jasmina touches my arm but I barely feel it. "And all because of the part you played in her life. Without you and Anisa, I don't want to think about what might've happened."

I don't want to either, but I can't help it. She would've died, and no one, especially a baby, should die because nobody loved them. With that thought comes another—one that shocks me but still feels right. It's a no-brainer when I really think about it. Since I love her more than anyone else, I should be the one to give her the life she deserves. The only way to do that is to take her away from here. I just have to figure out how.

6

I pay close attention to Cheryl's instructions on how to feed and burp the baby. I even watch while she changes her. After a while, she falls asleep in my arms. I feel like I never want to let her go. When Cheryl and Jasmina turn their attention to a stack of diapers that have fallen off a nearby shelf, I kiss the baby's forehead, silently vowing that I'll always be there for her.

After leaving the hospital, I make it to Anisa's church ten minutes early. I'll need her help with the baby. I only hope we're still friends.

The church is quiet, and peeking inside is impossible thanks to the windows being small and high up. Written in black paint at the very top of the building is the name of the church: GOD'S HOUSE OF BELIEVERS. Underneath that: DO GOD'S WILL AND YOU SHALL KNOW HIM.

I think about the baby and wonder if it was God's will that she was left behind. There's only one door with a small rectangular window covered with a shiny white curtain. This church is much different from the Catholic churches

I've been to. Those usually have two huge wooden doors that look kind of medieval. If I didn't know better, I'd think this door belonged to an apartment building.

I turn the knob but the door is locked. Just as I step away, a tall man wearing dirty jeans and a striped button-down shirt walks out. He leaves the door open while he pokes around in the trunk of a car. He's too busy to notice me.

I move to the church doorway and peer inside. Catholic churches smell like incense. Kind of tangy and sweet. This one reeks of something musty, like old wet books. The walls, painted light pink with yellow trim, look like an Easter egg. Other than that, this is just a big boring room filled with folding chairs. No colorful stained glass, no shiny wooden pews, and not a saint in sight. The only thing that gives it away as a church is the statue of Jesus standing on a pedestal in front of the room.

Not too far from the statue is a music stand like the ones they use in school during concerts. An open Bible lies across it. There's a guitar leaning on the wall in the corner and a small drum set standing next to it.

The trunk closes and I jump. "Can I help you?" the man in the dirty jeans asks. I don't know why, but I run past him without saying anything.

"Bible camp is canceled for today, if that's what you're looking for," he yells out.

I wait on the corner for twenty minutes just in case Anisa shows up, but she never does.

Hunger starts kicking around inside my stomach like I haven't eaten in days, so I walk to DeMarco's for a slice of pizza and a drink. I can't think on an empty stomach, and I do have five bucks to put to use.

A truck pulls up to DeMarco's just as I get there. It squeals to a halt and lets out a big puff of diesel fumes. Through the graffiti tagged along the side, I can just make out the name ACTION AUCTIONS.

The driver beeps his horn, and Enzo, the owner of De-Marco's, comes out to meet him wearing a white apron that barely fits around his large stomach.

"You Enzo?" the driver yells from the window.

"Yeah, that's me." His arms are covered in flour up to his elbows and pizza sauce is splattered on his white high-tops.

The driver steps out of the truck. "I got your *Star Wars* pinball machine here."

"All right!" Enzo says, then looks at me. "Hey, Lionel, I outbid a lot of big spenders last week down at the New Jersey Auction House for this very fine, very slick machine."

I know pinball games are old-school, but I can't help liking them. There's just something about the blinking score lights and corny music. I love how I can keep that little silver ball bouncing around for the longest time before it rolls down the middle. I like the feeling of the smooth red buttons on each side of the machine and the way I can use the paddles to hold the ball hostage until I'm ready to let it go. Anisa and I have been playing since we were eight years old, so

I'm up on my game. I know how not to get a tilt penalty and how to rack up extra points.

"Cool, Enzo, I can't wait to get my hands on that one. Darth Vader is going down."

Enzo pats my back as we walk inside. "I knew you'd like it. I was thinking about holding a tournament. What do you think of that? You want to be DeMarco's pinball king? We play against the guys from Tony's. The winner is looking at free pizza for six months."

"You know you don't have to ask me twice. You want me to put my pizza orders in now?"

"Show me the crown first."

"No problem. Just let me know when."

Inside, DeMarco's is pretty busy. I wait in line behind four people who order one of Enzo's newest creations, Lani slices. It's Hawaiian, with pineapple, ham, and cabbage on it. Anisa told him he couldn't pay her to eat that. I'd try it but not today. I'm not in the mood for anything new.

I give my usual order to Enzo: extra cheese and pepperoni.

"So what's going on with you, Lionel?" Enzo asks, smiling.

It seems like he's always in a good mood. "Nothing, you know, same stuff."

Watching the other workers behind the counter as they sprinkle shredded cheese on pizza dough gives me an idea. If I'm going to take care of the baby, I'm going to need a job. "Hey, Enzo, you need help around here?"

"Sorry, Lionel," he says, doling out the pepperoni. "I got all the bases covered, but I'll keep you in mind if anything comes up. You're good people. Oh," he continues while opening the oven, "your other half is already here. She's in the back."

"Anisa?"

"Yeah," he laughs. "You got another other half I don't know about?"

I can't believe my luck. I pay for my slice and while Enzo heats it up, I zigzag my way through the tables to the back room.

There's a lot of kids hanging out and talking in between bites, but it's easy to spot Anisa. She's playing a Spider-Man pinball game like her life depends on it. Dellie, a girl who lives in Mr. Brown's building, stands on one side cheering her on while Tyke is on the other side.

"Hey, Anisa, you're looking extra good today," Tyke says. "How about me and you hang out later?" He tries to put his arm around her but she shrugs him off.

"Leave her alone, Tyke," Dellie says.

"Come on, Anisa."

"Get away from me." Anisa pounds the buttons like mad, trying not to lose the game. "Go find somebody else to bother."

Just as I step over to Anisa, I notice Royce talking to a Puerto Rican dude, Andre, in the corner. With a gap between his teeth, he looks exactly like the football player Michael Strahan, only with a lighter complexion.

Andre's a senior in high school and he's pretty tough. He's already got some serious biceps like he spends every day lifting weights. I heard he started dealing weed in the ninth grade. Royce is looking all serious too.

A couple of girls are stomping around on DDR like they're auditioning for *Dancing with the Stars* or something.

"Anisa," I say, standing in front of Tyke. "I have to talk to you."

"Don't you see me standing here?" Tyke spits out.

"Yeah, but I need to talk to her in private," I say.

"Why? It's not like she's your girl or anything, right?"

"Man, whatever, Tyke. I don't have time for you."

Royce notices what's going on and calls Tyke over.

"I'll talk to you later, Anisa," Dellie says, walking away with a boy I never saw before.

Anisa doesn't take her eyes off the game. "You see Dellie's boyfriend? His name's Michael. She's crazy about him."

"Oh, that's nice," I say, relieved she's talking to me like nothing's changed.

"Tyke's been bugging me since he got here," Anisa says. "Thanks to Nelson, everybody thinks . . ." She takes a quick peek at me and lowers her voice. "That me and you did *it*."

"I know, but I already told Royce and Tyke that Nelson was lying."

"Doesn't seem to matter much to Tyke," Anisa says.

"Don't worry about him. He's just an idiot. But look," I say, changing the subject. "I want to talk to you about some things. First, what you said when I knocked on your door."

Before pulling the knob and releasing the pinball, she tightens her long ponytail like she's getting ready for battle. Lights flash and music sounds—she's scored free bonus points. "I'm sorry about that, Lionel, but you know how my mother is. You had to see her when Eva came home from school on the last day with two recognition awards. One was for English and the other was for math. She scored higher than anybody else in her school on her math Regents. My mom said she should've gotten at least three awards! Can you believe that? Poor Eva, you should've seen her face."

Of course I feel bad for Eva. I mean, her mother should be proud of her, not trying to make her feel terrible. Eva works harder in school than anybody else I know. She even volunteers in the soup kitchen at their church on the weekends. I've never told anybody but I've been crushing on Eva since I was ten. Anisa puts another quarter into the pinball machine. "Please tell me you didn't believe any of that stuff I said, did you?" she says. "I had to say something to make my mom stop going so crazy on me."

"I guess I just needed to hear you say it."

Her voice is almost a whisper. "I mean, don't you know how I feel about you? You're my best friend."

She avoids making eye contact and starts hitting the

flippers again. All the while I'm trying to figure out how to answer because something in her voice trips me up and gives me a funny feeling, almost like the feeling I had for the baby at the hospital.

The voice of the Green Goblin barks out an insane laugh, yanking me away from my thoughts. "Uh, yeah, I do. I was just being dumb, I guess."

She shoots me a pretty smile. Her teeth are perfectly straight even though she's never worn braces. "So, what else do you want to talk about?"

I lower my voice. "Are you okay after what they did to you at the hospital?"

She watches the last ball bounce back and forth on the bumpers, then against one of the paddles.

"Hit it!" I say.

Instead, the ball slowly rolls down the middle. Anisa's arms fall to her sides like she's just dropped something heavy. "Yeah," she says softly. "Thanks for sticking up for me, though. I'm glad you were there for me; it meant a lot."

I reach for her hand and her face brightens and I have a hard time looking away from her. "There's one more thing, Anisa. Maybe we should sit at a table first."

We find a quiet spot in the corner and Anisa waits for me to start. "I went to the hospital to see the baby today." I smile big and dumb. I don't ever remember feeling this proud. "They even let me feed her."

"What? You? I wish I'd been there to see that."

"Yeah, and I handled her just fine. The nurse even called me a natural."

"How is she? Is she okay?"

I nod. "But I'm going to make sure she's better than okay. I'm going to make sure she knows somebody loves her enough to take care of her. I'm taking her out of there."

Anisa wrinkles her nose and squints at the same time like maybe I'm speaking in another language and she has no idea what I'm saying. "Wait. What? Say that again."

"I want to take care of her. She deserves better—will you help me?"

"You mean you're going to KIDNAP her?"

Two of the girls waiting their turn on the DDR look over at us.

"Not so loud."

Just then Enzo walks over with my slice. "Not hungry anymore? Your pizza's been . . . Hey, Anisa, you look like you've just been contacted by aliens. You okay?"

"I'm fine, but I think Lionel's brain has been taken over by one." She cuts her big brown eyes at me.

"Oh, speaking of aliens," Enzo says. "I'm bidding on an *Independence Day* game tomorrow. You ever see that movie?"

I want to get back to planning with Anisa, and if Enzo knows I've seen it, he'll probably pull up a chair and never leave. "No, I haven't."

He puts my slice in front of me. "Too bad, it's a goody. Going to make a nice addition to the tournament too. And by the way," he says, "I was just talking it over with the guys and we decided the winner will get five hundred bucks."

I almost fall out of my chair. I'd be able to do a lot for the baby with that. "Are you kidding? The winner gets five HUNDRED dollars? Real cash? Not Monopoly money?"

"Aren't we full of questions." He points to his face with a stubby finger. "Do I look like I'm kidding?"

"Kind of," Anisa says.

"Yeah, well, Miss Wisenheimer, I'm not."

That money is as good as mine. "Count me in, Enzo. When's the tournament?"

"Not sure yet."

"You think it'll be soon?"

"I'd say definitely soon*ish*."

Enzo is being too vague for me and I have to concentrate on not raising my voice. "What? Like this week?"

"I haven't decided yet, sheesh."

I wait for Enzo to leave before picking up where we left off. "He might as well hand me that money now. You know how much it's gonna help with the baby?"

"Are you okay, Lionel? Like, have you hit your head or something?"

"Very funny. I'm fine."

The pizza sits in front of me practically calling my name. I offer Anisa a bite before tearing off a big piece.

"No, thanks, I had one already. So, getting back to your brilliant plan to kidnap the baby. How and why?"

"Why," I say through a mouth full of cheese. "I already told you. And how is what I need you to help me with."

"Me? No way, Lionel."

"They're going to put her in a foster home, Anisa. What if they turn out to be crazy people? What if they hurt her? It's not like that kind of stuff doesn't happen, you know. Remember Kevin from school?" Anisa shakes her head the whole time I talk. It's like she's not even listening to me.

"Can't you just think about it?" I say. "Jasmina said the baby will be there until Friday."

"You're really out of your mind. Where will you keep her?" Anisa says, losing patience. "You think your mother is just going to let you have her like she's a pet or something?"

"If I bring her home with me, Mom will want to keep her. I just know it," I say, thinking about Mom telling me how she felt when she saw me for the first time.

Anisa goes back to shaking her head. "Even if she did want to, which I seriously doubt, having a baby in the house is expensive—I should know. Mom sometimes has to decide between milk for Bella and lunch meat."

"The money from the tournament will help."

Anisa smacks her forehead. "Really? That's funny, because five hundred dollars is nothing when it comes to taking care of a baby."

"I know, I know. I plan on getting a job too."

Anisa jumps out of her seat and almost gives me a heart

attack. "Yeah, where, at Rikers? Because jail is exactly where they're going to throw your butt when they catch you."

I look around to make sure nobody is listening. "Calm down, I'm trying not to think about getting caught."

"You should be. This is stupid, Lionel. I mean, really stupid." Anisa crosses her arms over her chest. "Promise me you won't go through with it."

She's really starting to annoy me. I didn't expect her to get so crazy. I mean, she should want to make sure the baby stays safe too. "Fine, Anisa, I won't do it," I lie, finishing off my slice.

"You're lying."

"I'm not," I say in my most innocent voice.

"Lionel!"

"Relax, I'm telling you I won't do it, okay?"

After studying me for a few seconds, Anisa finally says, "Good!" She plops back in her seat exhausted. "I think you should still try to win the money, though. I have some quarters—want to practice?"

I stand and brush crumbs from my clothes. "No, I have to go, but thanks for *all* your help."

She ignores my sarcasm. "I'm just glad I could talk some sense into you."

"By the way," I say before leaving, "Mom arranged for me to take piano lessons again from Miss D., so I'll be spending a lot of time up there. You want me to ask her if you can take them too? That way we'll be able to hang out a little without your mother knowing."

"No, thanks," Anisa answers. "But good luck with *that.*"

The whole way back to Miss D.'s, I'm hoping I'm right about Mom wanting to keep the baby. It's a gamble, I know, but there's no other choice.

7

I was getting worried about you," Miss D. says when I finally get back to her apartment.

"Sorry I took so long."

"That's okay, you're here now." She hands me yesterday's newspaper and a bottle of vinegar. Does she want me to read or make a salad?

"What's this for?" I ask.

"For washing the windows."

"With this?"

"Yes, sir. It's the best. Won't leave any streaks at all." She pauses for a second, looking at her watch. "Why don't you start in the kitchen? I have to make a couple of calls."

"Okay."

After I pour some vinegar on a piece of newspaper, the room starts to smell like my feet after playing outside all day. I start with the top part of the window, but the sun is strong and it almost blinds me as I swipe the paper back and forth. Just when I think it's clean, I see more streaks and have to start all over again.

It takes me more than half an hour to finish, and that's just one window. When I'm done, Miss D. gives it what she calls the white-glove treatment. She studies the glass from every angle, then says, "Perfect, now you can start the windows in my bedroom."

The windowsill in Miss D.'s room looks like a mini forest. I have to move four big leafy plants to the floor. Before getting to work, I search the newspaper for the horoscope section. Mom reads hers every day even though she says nothing ever comes true. Maybe I'll get lucky. Maybe it'll give me a clue about what to do with the baby.

Use your imagination and you will impress someone you'd like to get to know better. Go over contracts carefully, making sure the fine print isn't something that will cause you problems at a later date. Love is heading in your direction, so plan something romantic.

It's way off base, especially the love part, but I do find a "buy one, get one free" coupon for diapers. I peek in on Miss D. before I tear it out of the paper and stuff it into my pocket. She's busy in her recliner dialing on a cordless phone. I don't mean to eavesdrop but I can't help it. "Why, hello, there," she says, sweet and syrupy.

She giggles like a little girl instead of a senior citizen. "We must be on the same wavelength because I was thinking about that too. Six thirty is perfect. See you then."

I duck back into the bedroom just as she clicks the phone off, and I wonder who could make her smile so much.

After a while, Miss D. comes in to see how I'm doing. "Good job, Lionel." She looks down to the courtyard and starts *tsk*ing. "I feel so sorry for what that girl's mother put her through."

Mom told her all about what happened at the hospital, so I know who she's talking about without even looking, but I do anyhow.

Anisa is busy pushing Bella around on a pink tricycle. Dellie tags along. I wonder what the baby will look like when she's Bella's age.

Royce and Tyke are sitting on the bench. Andre is off to the side standing real close to some skinny dude with sunken cheeks. They talk for a little while, and just before Andre walks away, he slips something into the dude's hand. You'd have to be stupid not to know he just sold him something.

I quickly go back to work on the window but Miss D.'s studying all the little kids who've come out to play.

I get to thinking of Anisa and what she said about babies being expensive, and I wonder what Miss D. did for work when her son was little, so I ask.

A smile spreads across her soft face. "You ever hear of Hattie Carthan?"

"No, never. Who is she?"

"Oh, she was a good friend of mine. I met her many years ago when we lived on the same block in Bedford-Stuyvesant."

"So you worked for her?"

Miss D. laughs. "No, no. I worked with her. She was older

than I was, but that chick was a doer." She points to a mark on the window. "You missed a spot."

"So what kinds of things did she do?" I ask, wiping the smudge.

"Well, with so many people coming and going, some good and some not so good, Bed-Stuy began to change for the worse. But none of that stopped Hattie. That's when she got the idea to start a block association. She thought it'd bring our neighborhood closer together, you know, maybe a little more like a family. Eventually, it did."

Then Miss D.'s face really livens up. Her eyes shine like she's watching a rerun of Saturday's fireworks show. "Hattie changed my life."

"She did? How?"

"Well, I was part of the reason she started the association. My husband—God rest his soul—had died two months before. Someone tried to rob him in the subway station not too far from where we lived. He died of a gunshot." Miss D. takes a big breath, then continues. "Hattie thought the association would help keep me busy. Can you believe only six other people showed up for our first meeting? I could tell Hattie was upset, only because I knew her so well."

I'm confused. "So your job was . . . ?"

"Oh, I'm sorry. I got off track, didn't I? My job was planting trees."

"What?" I try imagining Miss D. hauling trees around and digging holes.

"That and a lot more. Because of Hattie, do you know there's a wonderful magnolia tree with landmarked status still standing in Bed-Stuy? A man named William Lemken brought it there all the way from North Carolina in 1885!"

"Serious? I thought they only did stuff like that for old buildings."

Miss D. answers me from a chair in the corner of the room. "Usually, but Hattie was nowhere near usual. When she found out the city was going to cut that tree down, she jumped into action. That's just how she was, you know? At one point, she had us putting seeds into water balloons, then tossing them into abandoned dirt lots." Miss D. lets out a deep laugh. "By the time spring rolled into summer, those lots were full of the tallest sunflowers I'd ever seen. Oh, and the daisies! There must've been thousands of them."

"And that was your job? Throwing water balloons? I wouldn't mind doing that."

"Don't be silly. Taking that path led me to working in the Landmarks Preservation office. I even met the mayor!"

"That's cool, Miss D. So you still like planting things, right?" I ask, pointing to the mini forest.

"Very observant. Do you know when you speak nicely to plants, they flourish?"

I'm having a hard time believing that. "You mean like having a conversation with them?"

"Well, more like a one-sided one." She whispers, "They don't have much to say, you know."

We both have a good laugh over that.

By the time I'm finished with the windows, my hands look like raisins and stink of vinegar. I soak them in the bathroom sink for a few minutes, then find Miss D. and say good-bye.

"I'm looking forward to tomorrow's lesson, Lionel," she says as I step into the hallway.

"Don't forget, though, if you need something done again, I can do it, okay?"

"You got it." She closes the door.

It's four thirty and Mom gets home from the bank at six, so I make my way over to the basketball court.

There's a game already going when I get there. I spot Royce and Andre playing hard on opposite teams. Sweat is running off their heads like somebody sprayed them with a garden hose.

I get closer and notice Tyke sitting on the back of a broken bench with a group of guys I don't know. On the seat of the bench is a thick library book and a cell phone.

Tyke doesn't move over when he sees me, but I don't expect him to. The only available spot is at the end of the bench and it's nothing but a jagged wooden slat. I lean against the chain-link fence to watch the game.

Steven, a guy I recognize from school, bricks a shot against the rusty rim and everybody on the bench stands up and boos.

"Are you kidding?" Tyke says.

Some short dude in dreads goes after the ball, then feeds it to Royce, who's sweating through his shirt. He cuts like a madman, then crosses over, shoots, and makes it in.

Tyke jumps out of his seat again. "Ohhh, you see that? My boy's got nothing but net!"

The other team gets hold of the ball and passes it to one of the tallest players. He dunks it as easily as a cookie in milk.

The guy sitting next to Tyke with ashy legs and untied laces says, "Yo, that was crazy!"

Next, Andre steals the ball and takes off, holding on to his baggy jean shorts with one hand while dribbling with the other.

"Yo, dish it! Dish it!" somebody on the other side of the court yells.

Andre's not listening, though. Instead of passing the ball, he tries for the basket, but it's no surprise when it turns out to be just a killer air ball falling right into Royce's hands.

"What's up with Andre's game today?" the guy with the untied laces asks. "He's been cold this whole time."

"You might be bigger, but I'm badder and quicker!" Royce laughs.

Royce makes it right into the net. "Sa-*wishhhh*!"

You can tell by Andre's face he doesn't like being dissed. He gets all up on Royce even though we know Royce didn't mean nothing by it. "You think you funny?" he says.

Royce is shorter than Andre, so when he answers him, he has to look up. "No, just playing the game," he says.

They call a time-out when Andre starts chest-bumping Royce like he wants to fight, but Royce doesn't exactly look afraid because he isn't backing down.

All I know is that I'm glad that's not me. With all that muscle Andre's got, one bump from him and I'd be kissing the ground for sure.

Royce is mad. His lips disappear into a tight line but he just stares hard at Andre.

Andre's eyes bug out of his head. His shorts hang so low that if he starts throwing punches, they'll slide down to his ankles for sure. "How're you gonna be out here dissing *me* like that, huh?" Andre says. His light-skinned face is serious and scary.

Royce stands his ground and doesn't even blink.

I definitely couldn't be that brave going up against somebody like Andre. Just another thing added to Royce's list of assets. He's already got brains, clothes, a cell phone, and now, fearlessness.

Steven, the guy from school, tosses the ball toward Royce and Andre. "Let's just finish the game. You can take care of this later, Royce. When we're done."

Both Royce and Andre separate after that. Andre goes to the opposite side of the court, where his crew is hanging out. One of the guys hands him a water bottle. Andre takes a few gulps and hands it back. Royce jogs over to Steven and talks for a couple of minutes, then heads to the center of the court.

Finally the game gets going again and it's pretty uneventful. It ends with Royce's side winning.

Before walking off the court, Royce tells Andre he was just messing around. Then he asks, "We good?"

"Yeah, we cool. I was just hot 'cause some dude left me hanging and never showed."

That's when a little girl about two years old wanders over and stretches her arms toward Andre. "Daddy!"

Andre is a senior in high school, so he's got to be seventeen, eighteen years old. The same age as my parents when Mom got pregnant with me.

Royce comes over wiping sweat from his head. "What's up?" he says to me.

I go back to watching Andre hold his daughter and thinking about how good it felt to hold the baby in the hospital. Once Mom holds her too, everything will be all right.

A girl about Andre's age, wearing tight jeans and a black tube top, joins them.

Royce nudges me, forcing me to look away.

"Nothing. You know, same old, nothing."

He holds his hand out to Tyke. "My stuff."

As Tyke hands the cell and book over, I take a closer look. The book is called *The Color of Water* by James McBride and the phone isn't one of those cheap pay-as-you-go types of phones. It's one of the most expensive ones out there, and I should know because I did some research, thinking maybe

I could get a cell for my birthday. Mom said she couldn't afford it, though.

Tyke sees me checking out Royce's cell and has a good laugh. "Wish you had one, huh? Be careful, you might pop an eyeball staring like that."

I ignore Tyke because anything I say will let him know he got under my skin and I don't want to give him that satisfaction.

Royce checks his messages, then slips the phone into his pants pocket. "Don't know what you're laughing at. You want one too, but the way you're going, you'll never be able to get one."

Tyke nervously picks at his Nestlé Crunch–looking forehead. He should think about using some pimple cream. "You know I'm working on it."

"Apparently not hard enough." Royce sits on the bench and dusts off his sneakers.

That makes me look down at my own sneakers. There's more than dust on them. The ends of the laces have started to fray and some of the leather's peeled off of one toe. There's a gray spot where it should be white. "Royce, you got a job?"

"Yeah, I started a couple of months ago."

I stuff my hands into my pockets and try not to let on how badly I need one too. I ignore my messed-up sneakers and think of the baby. "Where?"

When he and Tyke eye each other quickly and respond

with "All over," I get a bad feeling. I think of Andre slipping something to that worn-out dude with the sunken cheeks.

I wait a couple of seconds to see if Royce is going to say something else, but he looks like he might never answer. Finally, he says, "Whatever I tell you has to stay between us, okay?"

I nod.

"I'm helping a friend out with his business. Just sometimes, though. Not like every day or nothing."

Before I say anything, I glance around to make sure no one is listening. "You talking about Andre, selling drugs, right?"

"Yeah, we've been delivering."

I think maybe I missed something because I've never heard of anything like that. "What do you mean?"

"Some of the other guys in the neighborhood are making a lot of money that way and Andre wanted to get in on it. He's looking for some extra help and I think you'd be good for it." He studies Tyke. "Way better than some other people, if you're interested."

I'm trying not to trip, to keep my reaction in check. But inside, I'm freaking out. I never thought somebody like Royce would ever have something to do with drugs. I mean, he does attend the George Academy with the rest of the smart kids. I thought a school like that would preach every day about how bad drugs are. I think about his cell and check out his sneakers. I would be lying if I said I wouldn't like to have those things too. But the truth is the baby would need a whole lot more.

"Hold up, Royce," Tyke starts. "You serious? Him better than me? He don't know anything about crack or Molly."

I heard about that stuff. Rappers sing about Molly all the time.

Royce shushes Tyke. "Be quiet. And, yeah, I'm serious. You're the one who brought your little cousin on a delivery, remember? I have no idea why Andre still lets you hang around."

"It was only that one time and my cousin didn't even know what was going on," Tyke says. "And Andre said he's thinking about giving me another chance."

Then, instead of getting in Royce's face, Tyke gets in mine. It's hard to take him seriously since he has to stretch up on his tiptoes to do it. "I know you can't do no better."

"It's not his fault you messed up," Royce says. "Andre needs somebody smart, honest, and on their game, like Lionel."

Tyke steps even closer to me. "Man, are you kidding? Him smart and honest? Yeah, right."

"He told us the truth about Anisa, right? He could've just let us believe whatever we wanted."

Other than Mom, nobody's ever called me smart or honest before and it makes me feel good. This is my chance to show Royce that I can handle myself too because that's what a job like this needs. "Man, Tyke, back off. Your breath is seriously humming. You been eating dog food or something?"

Royce busts out laughing while Tyke is steadily trying to burn a hole in me but I don't look away, not even for a second.

After seeing that I'm not about to back down anytime soon, Tyke says, "Man, whatever."

"Well?" Royce asks.

Even though I need the money, I'm not so sure I'm ready to get involved with anything having to do with drugs. "Can I think about it?"

Royce nods. "Yeah, just let me know."

It's wrong, but maybe I could just do it enough times to get the baby a few things like diapers and formula, then I could find something else to do. "Okay."

"I'm hungry, let's get some pizza," Royce says, scooping up his backpack off the ground.

I spent my last five dollars earlier. "Can't, I'm broke."

"No problem, I got it." Royce pats his pocket.

I almost ask him how much he gets paid but decide against it. Instead I just say thanks.

We walk past the bodega. The OPEN sign flashes red and green in the window like a Christmas decoration.

Tyke brings up how Andre was acting during the game.

"He was just getting out some aggression and whatnot," Royce says. "Wasn't no thing."

I hope I never have to deal with anything like that if I take the job.

"Oh, son, you see that car he drives now?" Tyke says. "It's not new but he fixed it up nice."

"Yeah, he's got big money, so he can afford something sweet like that."

"I'd take any kind of money, big or little!" Tyke answers.

"Always go for the big. Little won't do you much good," Royce says.

In DeMarco's, Royce orders a whole pie and we take it to the back to eat. I don't realize how hungry I am until I pull off a slice. Like always, the crust is crunchy and the sauce is a tiny bit sweet. Some black pepper and some garlic and I'm good to go.

We don't say anything until we're working on our second slices. Then I ask Royce what's up with the book he's carrying.

"It's on my summer reading list. I'm done with it, so I have to return it to the library. It was pretty good."

"You've already started your reading list?" I say.

"Yeah, and the author was born and raised in the Red Hook Projects."

"Wow, that's cool. What's the book about?"

"It's about the author's life and what it was like growing up with a white mom and a black dad."

I want to know more about the book but Royce starts

talking to a skinny Mexican kid who comes in. He's got the same dark complexion as Royce and straight hair that hangs almost into his eyes. His lips are red from eating a cherry Italian ice out of a paper cup.

"What's up, Sammy?" Royce says.

"Nothin', you know, just chillin'," the kid says, then slurps from his ice.

"You passed all your subjects?"

"Barely."

"Well, you come to me if you have any trouble in sixth grade, all right? I'll help you out."

"Cool, thanks." The kid goes over to where a bunch of girls are hanging out.

"What's that about?" I ask.

"I used to tutor him."

"Yeah," Tyke chimes in, pointing to the book. "Royce is one of those brainy boys."

"You like that school you go to?" I take a bite of my slice.

"Yeah, I do."

"So, tutoring was like a job? You get paid?"

Royce shakes his head while he chews on a big hunk of cheese. His lips have pizza grease on them. "No, I volunteered. I got this thing for teaching. My principal calls it a knack."

"Cool." I think if I had that kind of "knack" I'd charge money for it.

We play a few rounds of pinball after we're done eating, and before I know it, I'm late getting home. Hopefully I can still get there before Mom.

"Yo," Royce says before I leave. "Don't forget to let me know what you decide about that *job* I asked you about."

I almost chicken out, but I'm definitely going to have to help Mom out money-wise. "I already decided." I take a deep breath. "I'm in."

Tyke's big mouth hangs open while Royce writes down his cell number on a napkin. "That's what I'm talking about," he says.

When I get home, I'm surprised to see Mr. Owen sitting at the kitchen table having some iced tea with Mom. His Mets baseball cap sits on his thigh. I know he's friendly with my mom but Mr. Owen has never been in my apartment as far as I know.

Mom's hair is pulled back with a headband. She's still in her work clothes and is so mad her neck strains, showing off a thick vein on the side. It looks like it might pop. Mr. Owen tells her to calm down.

"Did I give you permission to go out after Miss D.'s?" she says.

"No." I look over at Mr. Owen, who's studying me. "But you didn't say I couldn't either." The last part pushes out louder than I meant.

"Now, that's no way to speak to your mother," Mr. Owen butts in.

"Lionel," Mom starts with a long sigh. "What has gotten into you?"

I know she doesn't want an answer to that and I'm glad

because I hardly know what's gotten into me. After I accepted Royce's offer, I somehow feel stronger. I mean, I'll be making money now. I'm not a little kid anymore. Mom continues the questioning. "I was worried. Where were you?"

"I was out."

Mr. Owen and Mom glance at each other.

"You think you're funny?" Mom says.

Her stockinged foot starts drumming the floor. That's my cue. I'm pushing her too far, so I back off. If I make her too mad it might hurt the baby's chances of staying here.

Mr. Owen's still staring. It makes me uncomfortable, like maybe he's got some weird ability to read minds.

"I was only watching a basketball game with Royce and Tyke, Mom. No big deal."

"Royce? Since when are you friends with him?"

"He asked me to hang out, that's all."

"Well, that's going to stop right now."

"What? Why?" I'm desperate. Without Royce, there is no job.

"Because I do not like the looks of him. The way he's got that other boy, Tyke, following him around doing stuff for him reeks of something and you will not be a part of whatever he's got going on."

"That's just how Tyke is, Mom. It doesn't mean anything."

"Don't fool yourself," Mr. Owen says, stirring a teaspoon of sugar into his glass. "Things always mean something, Lionel."

Mom crosses her arms and eyeballs me. "Mr. Owen is right, and I'll tell you another thing. You're not going to get the chance to find out what it means because starting tomorrow, after your piano lesson, you'll be too busy helping Mr. Owen do some work for Miss D." Her voice is heavy-duty loud. "And when you're done, you come straight home!"

It's like the walls have closed in, leaving me no space to move. I need to make that money. I grind my teeth in anger. Before I know it, I'm as loud as I want to be. "Why are you doing this to me?" *To the baby?* "I'm thirteen! I should be allowed to do what I want."

"If you don't start watching your tongue, I'm going to be doing a whole lot more to you! I'm trying my hardest to keep you out of trouble and you're not making it easy for me!" She looks away like the sight of me disgusts her. "Your dad didn't make things easy for me either."

I jam my fists into the pockets of my jeans to keep from punching something. I have to stop myself from crumpling the two pieces of paper I put in there earlier—the diaper coupon and the napkin with Royce's number on it. "Don't call him that!"

I hate what my father's done to us. Even though Mom works hard at the bank, there are still some weeks we barely have enough money for groceries plus our bills, because without his paycheck, things can get tight.

He turned me into one of those statistics people on television and the newspapers talk about. *A poor fatherless Latino kid* like that's all they see when they see me. I've never admitted this to Mom, because I know she tries her best, but it's embarrassing to fall into a category people expect you to be in. For once I'd like to give my father's phone number as an emergency contact at school or have him talk to the teachers at open school night. I want people to know I am more than a statistic.

"I don't have a father, *remember*?" I finish.

Instead of the angry storm I expected from Mom, all I see is hurt. But that doesn't stop me even though I know it should.

I turn my back. I don't want them to see the angry tears rising. "I hate him!"

Mom manages to keep her voice smooth. "I never want to hear you say that again. Hate doesn't take away from the hated, Lionel, just from the one doing the hating. Now, do you understand that you are to come straight home after Miss D.'s?"

When I don't answer, she loses whatever patience she has left and spins me around by my arm. "Look at me when I'm talking to you. I asked you a question."

"Yeah, Mom, I understand. But just so you know, I plan on being way better than my father. A better man, a better father, a better EVERYTHING!" I yank my arm away and duck into my bedroom, slamming the door.

I'm so wired I have to take deep breaths in order to calm down. I pace my small room until I'm dizzy, then curl up on my bed. I should've just kept my mouth shut. I need to stay on Mom's good side. If I don't, the baby will end up in that foster home, and the thought of letting her down is unbearable. She deserves a chance and I have to find a way to give it to her. I promised.

Mr. Owen knocks a couple of minutes later. "Lionel, can I come in?"

"No lock on the door, so it's not like I can stop you," I say from my bed.

He pokes his head in first. "I didn't ask about a lock. I'd like to talk to you; can I come in?"

"Yeah," I say into my pillow.

Mr. Owen makes himself comfortable on my desk chair and gets right to flapping his gums. "I think I might know how you're feeling, Lionel."

"What do you know about me?" *Nothing, that's what.*

"Oh, I know a lot of things."

"You think you know," I say. "But you don't know everything."

"No, not everything, but I do know my son might've felt some of the things you're feeling. Being thirteen isn't easy, is it?"

His son? I uncurl myself to get a better look at him. "You have a son? How come I never see him?"

Mr. Owen places his baseball cap on my desk. I watch as he slowly runs his fingers along the brim. He doesn't say anything right away and I think maybe he didn't hear me.

Just as I'm about to ask again, he finally says, "It's not always a parent who leaves."

"Yeah, well, that's what kids are supposed to do. Grow up and leave. Not parents."

"It wasn't exactly like he was grown. He ran away on the morning of his eighteenth birthday. I haven't seen him in twenty-five years. Don't even know if he's alive or dead."

That's hard for me to imagine. I mean, I don't see my father, but every once in a while he'll send us a money order and that at least lets me know he's alive—somewhere.

Mr. Owen doesn't look like the same man who was sitting at the kitchen table a few minutes ago. With the way his shoulders hunch over and the corners of his mouth hang down, it's like the sun has suddenly gone behind a cloud, leaving everything in a shadow.

I can't help but feel sorry for him. "Why didn't you stop him from going?"

"I don't think it would've mattered. Sometimes you just can't stop a person from doing what they want." He points to me even though we're supposed to be talking about him. "The only thing you have any real control over is what *you* do and how *you* respond."

I watch Mr. Owen and wonder if this is the way a father is supposed to talk to his son. He didn't have to come in here and talk to me like this but he did anyway. After Mr. Owen leaves my room, he hangs around a little longer talking quietly to Mom. Then the only sound I hear coming from the living room is Lionel Richie singing his corny heart out about dancing on some dang ceiling.

We eat dinner a little while later. Mom's wearing her glasses and her eyes are red and puffy like she's been crying. I don't like that I was the cause of that.

"I'm sorry," I blurt out.

"Me too," she says quietly.

We clean up, then Mom goes into her bedroom to change. I take out my baby album and sit on the couch with it. On the first page there's a photo of Mom standing beside my father's beat-up car. Mom's pregnant and wearing a bright yellow-and-black-striped dress, white shoes, and instead of a smile, she's got a serious look on her face. I've seen this picture lots of times, and even teased her about what she was wearing. I told her she looked like a huge bumblebee. But now that I know what Mom was going through back then, I don't see anything funny.

I stare into my father's face wondering what he might've looked like when he was my age. He didn't stick around long enough to tell me himself. Sometimes I wonder about stupid things like whether or not I got my big feet from him or how old he was when stubble started showing up on his face. Other times I worry about more important stuff like whether or not it's in my blood to run off and not care about the people I leave behind.

Mom comes out and sits beside me. "Your father loved that old Toyota Celica." She smiles. "It left us stranded more times than I'd like to remember."

The next photo is of me still in the hospital. Mom says the hospital always takes a photo of a newborn baby, usually right before they discharge you.

"My aunt Loida crocheted that little outfit for you. When I got you home, you had a rash from it. I didn't tell her, though, because I thought it would hurt her feelings."

I've heard this story before, but I don't stop Mom, because it seems like she's enjoying the telling.

On the next page is a photo of my father holding me on his first Father's Day. Instead of looking at the camera, he's looking at me like I'm the most important thing in the world to him. I wonder how that could've changed. It takes a long time before Mom turns the page.

Going through the album mostly feels good but it makes me sad to think of how everything is so different now.

We take our time and when we get to the last photo Mom says she's beat. She stands, then kisses me on the head.

"Good night, honey."

"Mom," I say before she heads into her bedroom. "After you told Grandma you were pregnant, what did she do?"

"Well, she didn't kill me." She laughs. "But she yelled for about a month straight. I wasn't even allowed to say your father's name around her."

"And after that?"

"She barely spoke to me at all then, and suddenly I missed the yelling. But after we got married and you were born, things got better. She was there when I needed her the most."

"Are you sure you're not sorry you had me?"

She sits back down. "No, not for a second. You were my gift. Still are."

I hope she feels the same way about the baby when I bring her home.

We say good night for real and each go into our bedrooms. It's ten thirty but I'm not sleepy. My mind is going around and around, thinking about how I'm going to get the baby out of the hospital. I've heard stories of babies being taken on the news. The person usually dresses like a nurse and just walks out with it. I remember that little room Jasmina took me into when I went to see the baby. Maybe there were nurses' scrubs piled on the shelves along with the polka-dotted gowns. I'll go back to the hospital tomorrow to check it out.

I start getting sleepy but I can't seem to shut my mind off because I start thinking about how my father used to walk me to school every morning and tell me lame knock-knock jokes. I'd laugh anyway because I didn't want him to feel bad. He even used to make my lunch and give me an extra snack when Mom wasn't looking. It didn't matter if it was around Halloween or not. He'd wink at me and whisper, "Trick or treat," then throw in a Kit Kat or a bag of M&M's.

My throat feels like it's shrinking and I have trouble swallowing. I don't let any tears come down, though. My father doesn't deserve them, just like I didn't deserve how he fooled me into believing he loved me. Still, I can't help putting his T-shirt on over mine before getting into bed and falling into a restless sleep. It's not long before I start to dream.

A fat black cat chases me and Anisa through the lot.

"But I thought you liked cats!" I yell.

"Not this kind. It's too big."

The cat is now a tiger and it's right behind us. I can feel its hot breath on my neck. With outstretched claws, its thick paws thud on the ground behind us, kicking up dirt and bits of rock. Every step becomes a thunderclap. "Hungry! Hungry!" it roars.

"In here," I say, flinging the door to the Porta-Potti open.

After the door slams behind us, we slide the lock over to OCCUPIED.

Everything inside is exactly the same as when we found the baby.

Outside, the tiger claws at the door. My legs wobble so much I have trouble standing.

Anisa points to a crumpled T-shirt on the floor. "What's that?"

A tiny wrinkled foot pokes out from underneath the shirt. I throw the shirt aside. "A baby girl!" I say.

This time, I'm the one to pick up the baby. "We have to feed her. Let's take her home!"

But Anisa doesn't want to. "No, the father will come get her. Don't worry."

The baby snuggles into the crook of my neck. She's warm and soft, and smells fresh and clean like a just-washed towel.

Now the tiger throws himself against the door, shaking the Porta-Potti, and I'm afraid it's going to tip over. "Hungry!"

I kiss the baby's silky smooth hair. "I'll protect you."

The minute Anisa yells, "GO AWAY!" the tiger gives one more roar, then bursts through the door.

I wake up in a panic worried I've lied to the baby about protecting her. I sit up and take a couple of deep breaths before remembering my plan for the hospital scrubs. That makes me feel a little better.

Maybe Mom had trouble sleeping too, because she's in the living room listening to Lionel Richie, and every now and then she picks a part to sing along with.

I see the tears you cry.
I see the pain that's in your eyes.

The volume is low but I can still hear every word. If I wanted to, I could sing with her. These lyrics have been burned inside me for a long time and usually I think they're real corny but not tonight.

I lie back down wondering if the baby's parents are sleeping right now and if they're dreaming about her too. I wonder if my father ever dreams of me.

When the music stops and I'm sure Mom has gone to sleep, I take the napkin out of my pants pocket, sneak into the kitchen, and dial Royce's cell.

It's twelve thirty and not a hint of sleep in his voice. "Yo."

I whisper into the kitchen phone. "It's Lionel. Can I start that job tomorrow?"

"Yeah, we got something poppin' at one o'clock on the corner of DeMarco's."

9

When I get to Miss D.'s the next morning, Mr. Owen answers the door, surprising me. He's wearing his Mets hat and holding a pack of lightbulbs.

"You're late." He sounds like he's been waiting for days instead of twenty minutes.

"Yeah, sorry, my alarm clock didn't go off on time."

"Didn't go off, or you just didn't get out of bed?" His dark eyes have a hint of a smile in them and I don't know how to answer.

He's right, but I don't know why I have to be on time for a piano lesson I don't even want. I nod anyway.

"Just try to be on time from now on. It's not nice leaving Miss D. waiting on you."

Miss D. comes out from the kitchen wearing a tie-dyed skirt, a shirt that says GIVE PEACE A CHANCE, and shiny red sandals. Her gray hair, gathered on top of her head like a perfectly baked cinnamon roll. Wisps of hair hang down like ribbons on a birthday present. She's even wearing makeup. Pink lipstick to match the pink on her cheeks. "Well, here's my star student. Fingers all warmed up on this beautiful Tuesday morning, Lionel?"

"Star? I'm more of a meteor who's about to crash and burn on that piano."

When Miss D. smiles, her eyes crinkle into little half-moons behind her glasses. She takes a seat on the bench, then motions for me to sit next to her. "Now, don't think like that. You'll get it. You just wait and see."

Her voice is so cheery I almost believe her.

Mr. Owen studies Miss D.'s peace sign earrings. "Glad to see you're enjoying them. They look beautiful on you."

"Well, you have very good taste," she says sweetly.

It's nice they have each other and I can't help but smile.

Mr. Owen tells us to have fun, then walks toward Miss D.'s bedroom. "I'll just finish setting up your curtain rods."

I spot the wooden sticks Miss D. had me use to bang on the piano yesterday. "You need any help in there, Mr. Owen?"

"No, I'm good for now, but maybe later."

"Let's get cracking," Miss D. says.

We've only been sitting at the piano for thirty minutes but it seems like forever. It's impossible to concentrate on anything Miss D. says, and even worse, I'm trying not to think how I need to be out there to meet Royce at one o'clock. I glance at my watch again. Eleven fifty.

"Everything all right?" Miss D. asks.

"Yes, why?"

"You've been scooting around on the bench an awful lot and now you're looking at your watch. Something on your mind?"

She'd probably faint right on the spot if I told her what's on my mind. Helping Royce deliver drugs for Andre, and in Anisa's words, kidnapping. The thought of being locked up in Rikers scares me, but I can't think about that. All I want to do is finish what we started—rescuing the baby, that's all.

I press some of the keys but they're not the right ones. "No, I'm fine."

"Glad to hear it. Now, start over and remember to put all your fingers to work."

At twelve thirty, when Miss D. is finally tired of listening to me massacre "When the Saints Go Marching In," she declares the lesson over. "Tomorrow, not only do your fingers need to be warmed up, but your mind does too. You need to concentrate and not be so worried about the time. I don't want any more scooting, and it might be a good idea to leave your watch at home!"

As soon as the piano goes silent, Mr. Owen is in the living room with us.

"All done?"

"For now," Miss D. answers.

"Good, I could use some help after all. Come with me, Lionel. I need to get something from my apartment."

When no one is watching, I peek at my watch. I've got thirty minutes before I have to meet Royce and I still haven't worked out how I'm going to get out of here.

Mr. Owen opens the apartment door. "Well?"

I have no choice but to follow him.

Mr. Owen's place is almost as full of plants as Miss D.'s. A tall cactus sits in a green pot near the window. It's just one tall trunk and doesn't resemble any of the ones I've seen in cartoons. Those have three pieces. One main trunk, like Mr. Owen's, plus a piece on each side looking like arms. Mr. Owen's does have lots of thorns, though, and that's how I know for sure it's a cactus. I can even see them from where I'm standing. I can't imagine how Mr. Owen waters it without impaling himself on one.

I check out the place a little more while Mr. Owen walks toward his bedroom. It's cleaner than I expected it to be. I thought bachelors didn't care about things like neatness. The floors are spotless and there's nothing out of place anywhere—even the pillows on the couch line up like nobody ever sits on it.

"It's back here," Mr. Owen says from the bedroom doorway.

As I head in his direction I see a frame hanging on the wall. Inside is a medal shaped like a cross. It hangs from a red, white, and blue ribbon. "What's this?" I say, stopping in front of it.

Beside me, Mr. Owen straightens out the collar of his checkered shirt. Then he pulls his shoulders back so he looks taller. "This is my most prized possession. It's a medal I received while serving in the Vietnam War as a helicopter medic. I was twenty-three years old when I enlisted, a little older than some of the guys I served with." He looks real serious and for a minute I think he might salute the medal but he doesn't. "It's called the Distinguished Flying Cross."

The closest I've come to knowing anybody who's been in a war is a kid who goes to my school. He's got a cousin who lost both legs fighting in Afghanistan. "Wow, why'd they give it to you?"

"Well, I suppose I worked for it. Almost got my rear end blown up earning it too!"

"Serious? What happened?"

"Our job was to get the wounded out of the battlefield. I can remember this one time we were picking up some soldiers on a dust-off mission—"

"Wait," I say. "What's a dust-off mission?"

"We called them dust-offs because when the helicopter took off, the dust kicked up something fierce, making it almost impossible for us to see. That's when the Viet Cong knew we were the most vulnerable and fired at us."

"Oh, man. But didn't you have guns too?"

"Of course we did, but my hands were always preoccupied with trying to save someone's life. I took my chances, all the while praying that we'd get away alive."

"So, you're, like, a hero," I say, watching his dark-skinned face closely.

He stares at the medal and doesn't say anything. It's like he's remembering all the people he saved.

"Were you scared?" I ask.

"Yes, indeed. We all were. Every second of every day meant possibly the end of our young lives."

I won't be getting any medals, but when I leave the hospital with the baby, I'm going to have to be as brave as Mr. Owen was. "You'd be surprised what you're capable of when it comes down to the nitty-gritty," he continues.

With everything I'm about to do, including working for Andre, I know it's the truth. I don't think I can get any more nitty-gritty.

We both stare at the medal for a few more seconds while I think about Mr. Owen on the battlefield saving lives. There's no question about what kind of man he is. Then I wonder about my father and what kind of man he considers himself to be.

I help Mr. Owen get the ladder out of his closet, then we head back to Miss D.'s.

Mr. Owen sets up the ladder in the bedroom. From the top of it he hands me a burned-out bulb from the ceiling fan. "Hand me a new one, please."

While he screws the bulb in, he says, "So, you've made some new friends."

After learning about Mr. Owen's medal, I'm worried about what he thinks of me. "Uh-huh."

"You know how to speak English, and 'uh-huh' is not an English word. It's the sound cavemen used."

"Yes, I made new friends."

"You know what my motto is, Lionel?" He doesn't give me a chance to answer. "Friend up." He pokes a thumb toward the ceiling.

"What does that mean?"

"Always make friends with people you can look up to. People you can admire, not ones that'll drag you down along with them." Mr. Owen steps off the ladder. "The only way anybody has ever gotten anywhere in this world was to friend up. I imagine that's how the cavemen did it."

I know he's talking about Royce and Tyke but I just answer with a simple "Okay."

"Are you hungry?" Miss D. says from the doorway. "I made fresh blueberry muffins early this morning."

"They're the best muffins I've ever eaten, and considering how old I am, that's saying something!" Mr. Owen says.

The thought of the muffins makes my stomach grumble, especially since all I had before leaving my apartment was a handful of cereal.

"Excuse me," Miss D. says teasingly. "I take offense to that since we're the same age!"

That's weird because Mr. Owen looks a few years

younger than Miss D., even with gray hairs sprouting from his face.

Mr. Owen matches Miss D.'s playfulness with, "No, you've got to be much younger than I am." Their smiles linger longer than they should, then Mr. Owen apologizes for insulting a beautiful lady.

The phone rings and Miss D. picks it up. "Yes, he's here safe and sound."

She listens for a minute, then says good-bye.

"That was your mother, Lionel. She wanted me to tell you she's got a meeting after work tonight, so she'll be a little late."

Mr. Owen clears his throat. "About those muffins—why don't we let the boy do some more work before eating? That way, he'll have a chance to work up an appetite." He hands me a screwdriver without even looking my way. "The knobs on Miss Dorothy's dresser drawers and night tables need to be tightened up."

It's obvious that he's thinking about Miss D. and not about me or my appetite. I get to work anyway.

I tighten every single screw, even the ones that aren't loose, all the while trying to come up with an excuse to get out of here so I can meet up with Royce. I have ten minutes and I can't be late on the very first day. He just might decide to give the job back to Tyke.

When I come out of the bedroom, Miss D. and Mr. Owen are holding hands across the kitchen table. It takes them a minute to notice I'm in the room. I can't help grinning.

"Done already?" Mr. Owen asks, moving his hand away.

"Yes," I say.

"Good, now sit down and eat," Miss D. says, pouring me a glass of ice-cold milk. She puts the biggest muffin on a plate and sets it down, but there's no time to eat.

It's almost one o'clock. I ignore my stomach. "No, thank you, I'm not hungry. Don't you need me to run errands for you, Miss D.?" I look at the almost-empty milk container. "Don't you need more milk?"

Miss D. says she's got another in the fridge, but Mr. Owen watches me closely. "So, this Royce. You like being his friend?"

I glance at Miss D.'s small clock on the wall above the table. There's no way I'll be able to get to Royce now, so I give in to the fact that I won't be making any money today. I still have to get to the hospital, though, to check for the nurses' scrubs.

Sitting across from Mr. Owen, I bite my muffin and take my time chewing. "Yes," I say after swallowing.

"I don't think it's a good idea," Mr. Owen says flatly.

He might know a lot of things but I doubt he knows what's good for me. I've barely been around him.

"Those boys are bad news and that's not friending up."

"We don't know that for a fact, William," Miss D. interrupts, and I'm hoping that'll be the end of it.

"Oh, as far as I'm concerned it's pure fact." Mr. Owen takes a long sip of his coffee and studies me over his mug.

Finally he says, "Feel like talking about what's going on . . . exactly?"

"I don't know what you mean," I croak.

Mr. Owen looks at me sideways. "You sure about that?"

I nod, then stuff another piece of muffin into my mouth.

After an hour under Mr. Owen's watchful eye—vacuuming out the bottoms of two closets, moving Miss D.'s television from one table to another, and reorganizing everything underneath the kitchen sink, I'm finally done. If I can come up with a way to leave Miss D.'s, first I'll try to find Royce and beg him to give me another chance, then I'll go to the hospital. I just have to make sure Mom doesn't find out.

Mr. Owen stands outside the bathroom while I'm washing up. I hope he doesn't try to get me talking again. I should've locked the door, or at least closed it.

"I know you must think I'm a hard dude, huh?"

Dude? He's too old to be a dude. "Um . . . ," I squeeze out through the towel as I dry my face.

"I just don't want to see you go down the wrong path." He sticks his hand into his pants pocket and jingles some change. "Around here, *that* path is so beat-up and worn-down, it's sad."

I continue to rub my face with the towel like it's still wet. I think about the job Royce offered me, and I know that's the path Mr. Owen is talking about, but I don't intend to stay on that path long. Just enough to help Mom get some of the big things, like a crib, a stroller, and whatever else we're going to need in the beginning. I'll have to lie to Mom about where the money came from. Maybe I'll tell her Enzo hired me. I'll just have to hurry up and find another job before she finds out the truth.

His voice gets all soft, like when you're remembering something bad. He didn't even sound like that when he talked about being shot at in the war and not being able to shoot back.

"I know all too well what happens to a boy who chooses *that* path, Lionel."

Miss D. is moving around in the living room and I wish I was out there with her.

Curiosity gets the best of me. "Your son?" I ask, taking a peek at him.

"Yes. He started on that path when he was fourteen years old. He'll be forty-three this year." He sighs heavily.

"So, what did you do when you found out what he was up to?" I ask.

"Well, I tried everything I could think of. I tried scaring Thomas by having a police officer talk to him, I grounded him, put a lock on the phone so he couldn't call his so-called friends, and even changed my work hours so I could pick him up after school." Mr. Owen shakes his head. "I'm not proud of this but I lost my temper a few times and used my belt to hit him." He pauses and the corners of his lips turn down. "I think that might be what really pushed him to leave."

I can't imagine Mr. Owen hitting anyone, especially his son.

I have no idea what to say. If Mom ever hit me with a belt, I don't know what I'd do.

Before I know it, Mr. Owen's gone.

10

After I'm finished in the bathroom, I find Mr. Owen and Miss D. talking in the kitchen. Miss D. is almost the same height as Mr. Owen, thanks to her shiny sandals, and when she gently touches the side of his face, he kisses her hand.

I don't want to embarrass them, so I quietly walk back to the bathroom and noisily close the door. In the kitchen, Mr. Owen doesn't seem so sad anymore.

Mr. Owen sits at the table with a deck of playing cards. He shuffles them like an expert, quickly flipping the cards over and over again. Finally, he cuts the deck in half. "Now, don't be jealous of my skills . . ."

I try holding my laugh in but it sneaks out anyway. "Um, I'll try not to."

In his best Bill Cosby voice he says, "Now, that's a mighty fine idea. You do that, young man."

Miss D. laughs, taking a seat across from Mr. Owen. "William, you know being a show-off isn't cool."

"Maybe I'll teach you sometime, if you're lucky."

"And if you're lucky, I'll let you."

All the playfulness goes out of Mr. Owen's voice. "I'm already lucky."

Miss D. blushes, and it's not just the pink makeup on her cheeks.

Suddenly Mr. Owen's attention is turned toward me. "Hey, Lionel, you have a girl?"

Miss D. slaps Mr. Owen's hand jokingly. "Don't. You'll embarrass the boy."

Now I'm the one to blush. I've never had a girlfriend and it's not like girls are lining up for a date. Nobody wants to be seen with Mr. Potato Head's clone. "No," I say.

"Well, what about you and Anisa? You two seem to be an item," Mr. Owen says.

Maybe I should start wearing a sign that says Anisa is not my girlfriend.

"No, we're just friends."

"Well, there's nothing wrong with that, Lionel," Miss D. says, cutting her eyes at Mr. Owen. "You're a handsome boy. I'm sure there are plenty of girls who'd love to be your girlfriend."

"There is this one girl . . . ," I say, thinking about Eva.

I've got Mr. Owen's full attention. He pulls out a chair for me and I sit. "Go on," he says.

"Well, I have a crush on her. She's older, though, and would probably never go for somebody like me."

"You never know, Lionel. You're mature for your age." Miss D. takes off her glasses and cleans them with a tissue from her pocket. "Don't sell yourself short," she finishes.

"Yeah, but at least not knowing for sure leaves me with some hope. That's what Mom says when she plays the lottery and doesn't check the tickets right away. She calls it 'living in maybe.'"

"I like that, Lionel. Your mom's a pretty smart cookie," Miss D. says.

"This girl is smart too," I say, thinking about Eva's awards that Anisa told me about. "Out of everybody in her school, she scored the highest on her math Regents."

Mr. Owen pushes the brim of his Mets cap higher. "Smart is good. Does this girl have a name?"

I'm not sure I want them to know. It's not that they'd laugh at me or anything, but they might tell me it's a lost cause. And I don't want to lose living in maybe.

When I don't answer, Mr. Owen asks, "Well then, what else can you tell us about this mystery girl?"

I think about Eva's wavy light brown hair and dark, intense eyes and how sometimes when she looks at me, I feel like an open book. Like maybe she can read my mind.

But I don't think that's the kind of information Mr. Owen is looking for. Then I remember something I saw Eva do once while I was helping her carry her textbooks after school.

"She's not afraid to stand up for people," I say.

"So she's courageous," Mr. Owen says, smiling. "That's a great quality to possess. Tell us about that." He leans forward with his elbows on the table.

Too bad Anisa doesn't think I'm being courageous for wanting to take the baby. She just thinks I'm stupid.

"William, why are you giving Lionel the third degree?" Miss D. says.

"Just exercising his conversational skills. But if you don't want to talk about this, Lionel . . ."

"No, it's okay. I don't mind." I never get the chance to talk to anyone about Eva and it feels good. "Once there were a bunch of older kids pushing another kid around. She saw them before I did and ran over to break it up. They were about to throw him into the street. If it hadn't been for her, the kid would've been hit by a bus and maybe even killed."

Miss D. gasps.

"Then we both walked the kid home and told his mom what happened."

I glance at the wall clock—uh-oh, it's already four. I totally forgot the time. I've got to get to the hospital, so I cut the conversation short. "And that's basically it."

"Well, I hope your mystery girl finds out you like her and gives you a chance," Miss D. says.

"Yeah," Mr. Owen adds. "Sounds to me like she's a mighty fine girl."

Then Mr. Owen picks up the deck of cards and asks if I'd like to play rummy with them.

"Um . . . I should be getting home," I say, standing and stretching out my legs. "Besides, I don't know how to play."

"Sit down, it's easy. I'll teach you."

I'm itching to get out of here. I have to see about those scrubs. "No, thanks."

"You're afraid I'll kick your behind, huh?" Mr. Owen asks, shuffling the cards again.

"What? No way."

"Then have yourself a seat and get ready for a beat-down."

"Don't listen to him, Lionel," Miss D. says. "What he doesn't know is that I'll be doing the behind-kicking around here today."

Mr. Owen and Miss D. start teasing each other. I like being with them and really don't want to go but I have to.

Just as I'm about to leave the apartment, there's a knock on the door.

I answer it and find Anisa. Right away I know something is wrong because her cheeks and neck are splotchy.

I step into the hallway, closing the door behind me.

"I figured you'd be here." She drags me away from Miss D.'s door, then lowers her voice. "There's something wrong with Eva and I don't know what to do."

"What're you talking about? What happened?"

"I don't know, Lionel. After my mother went out with Bellita, I found Eva mumbling in her sleep. I had a hard time trying to get her up and when she finally did wake up, she started crying. I asked her what was wrong but she wouldn't answer me. She only cried harder, so I sat with her and that's . . . when I saw blood all over the sheets."

"What? Is she cut or something?"

"No! I mean I don't think so. She won't get up and she won't let me call my mother."

Anisa doesn't cry easily but now the tears fall fast. "You have to come help me."

"Okay, wait for me here." I take a few deep breaths before opening Miss D.'s door and peeking inside.

"Is it all right if I run down to Anisa's and help her with something?"

Mr. Owen starts to say no but Miss D. cuts him off. "As long as you'll be right back and you promise not to leave the building."

"I promise!"

We don't wait for the elevator and make it down to the second floor in record time.

With Eva's bedroom windows closed and the shades pulled down, it's hard to tell it's daylight outside. The room is warm and stuffy like how the gym at school feels after a basketball game.

Anisa turns on a lamp and accidentally knocks a thick book to the floor with a loud thump. *The Country's Top 100 Colleges.* Some pages are dog-eared and the cover is bent and worn like Eva has read it a million times, which wouldn't surprise me. The awards she got in school are tacked to her wall.

Eva, still curled up underneath a purple quilt, is eerily quiet and still. I gently nudge her but she doesn't stir. "Eva?"

Still nothing. Not even after nudging her again.

Anisa pushes me out of the way. "Evalisse!"

Finally, there's movement beneath the quilt. Her voice is small. "Just leave me alone."

"I will, but only after you tell me what's wrong," Anisa says.

"You can't help me. Nobody can."

I start to tell her that she's wrong, that I'm here and can help her, but she starts talking to God. I can't call it praying exactly, because people usually pray for good things and this definitely isn't good.

"Dear Lord, I am not worthy of your love or forgiveness. Please, please, let me die!"

Anisa runs out of the room, leaving me alone to try to make sense of Eva's words. I know God wouldn't let Eva die, or anyone else, just because they ask—but hearing her beg Him like that freaks me out. "Don't say that—I can help you, Eva. You just have to tell me what's going on."

When Anisa comes back she's carrying a cordless phone. Her hands shake as she tries to dial. "That's it, you're talking crazy and you're bleeding . . . I'm calling 911."

Eva pulls the quilt off her head. My heart breaks at the sight of her swollen, worried eyes. Her skin is pale and her lips are dry and chapped. "No! Not 911." Her voice is raw and her face wet with tears. "Anisa, please, Mami will kill me."

Anisa falls to her knees to the side of the bed. "Kill you? Oh, my God. What did you do, Eva? What happened?"

I wish this was a prank but something deep inside tells me it's not.

Eva stares off into space and I almost cover my ears. I don't want to hear what she has to say because I think I already know.

"No," I say.

Anisa's voice quivers. "You're scaring me. Why do you think Mami is going to kill you? You never do anything bad." She gives a little nervous laugh. "Come on, you're her favorite, remember?"

Eva rolls away from us and speaks quietly toward the wall. "Because the baby you saved, it's . . . she's mine."

11

The room fills with an invisible thing. It's big and dark and threatens to steal away every good feeling I've ever had about Eva.

Anisa jumps to her feet. "You're lying!"

Every part of me wills Eva to admit what Anisa says is true. That she's just making this up. But she's quiet and as still as she was when we first came in. The invisible thing is winning, and Anisa must feel it too because she hops onto the bed, kneeling close to Eva. In one move, she flings the quilt to the floor. "Why would you say something so stupid?"

The only answer she gets is Eva's wail. "Because it's true." She struggles to sit up. Even in the dim light I see fear and worry etched on her pretty face. On the quilt there is a large circle of fresh blood.

In an instant I know what it means to have a broken heart. This is going to change everything for Eva, her future and her dreams.

Anisa gives Eva's shoulder a hard shove like maybe it'll help loosen the truth from Eva's mouth. "No, you're lying!"

This is too big for me. Too big for any of us.

Anisa hides her face in her hands. Her sobs hammer away at my ears in rhythm with my own heartbeat. Mr. Owen's words about fighting in the war—and how you'd be surprised by what you're really capable of—repeat in my head.

I step closer to Anisa. "Look at her. She's telling the truth."

Anisa moves her hands away from her face just enough to see Eva. "Oh, my God." She grabs the small garbage can on the side of Eva's desk and vomits into it.

"Do you think the baby will ever be able to forgive me?" Eva asks after Anisa puts the garbage can down. Anisa nods but it's not very encouraging. Feeling like you weren't good enough just doesn't go away and forgiveness might not ever happen.

I take Eva's hand. It's burning up. I feel her forehead, which is even hotter. "She's running a fever. Anisa, when is your mother coming home?"

"Not until later. Eva, we have to call Mami."

"No, no. I'm okay. Just help me get up so I can take a cool shower."

Once Eva settles into the bathroom, Anisa changes Eva's sheets and throws the dirty ones down the garbage chute in the hallway. Even though there is so much to say, we're quiet the whole time, like maybe if we don't talk about it, it won't be real.

Finally, Anisa breaks the silence. "We saved my niece, Lionel."

She's right and now more than ever, I need to go on with my plan. I think about how scared Mom was when she was pregnant and I know that Eva really didn't mean to leave her baby. She was just afraid. Once I get the baby back to her, she'll realize everything will be okay, just like it was for Mom. "Will you help me take her from the hospital now?"

She pushes her dark hair away from her sweaty face. Her words sound unsure and don't convince me of anything. "No . . . that's crazy." Then, after a second, "She might not even be there anymore."

"She'll be there until at least Friday, remember?"

"Can't we go to the hospital and tell them the baby is my niece and she belongs home with her family?"

"It doesn't matter what we say. They're not going to just hand the baby over to us. My solution is the only one, Anisa."

"I'm too scared, Lionel. I don't think I can do it and maybe you shouldn't either. If you get caught . . ."

But my mind is already made up. I have to give Eva the chance to be forgiven. "I've got to at least try."

I leave the building without letting Miss D. or Mr. Owen know. There's just no other way.

Outside it's hot and sticky, just like any other July day in New York City. But I'd be lying if I said that's the only reason sweat trickles from every part of me. I'm nervous. Thinking about taking the baby and actually doing it are different things. I'm just hoping that when Anisa's mother and Eva see the baby they'll feel the same way Mom did when she first saw me.

I'm still about fifteen blocks away from the hospital when a black Nissan Altima pulls up alongside me. It's a real nice one with cool rims and tinted windows. "What happened? Thought you were meeting me today," Royce says from the passenger seat. He's wearing shades I can see my reflection in.

Andre is sitting in the driver's seat. He's got a diamond earring in his ear and I wonder if it's real. His hair is cut close like he just got a shape-up. All the lines are neat and sharp. He leans over, checking me out from top to bottom. "This Lionel, the guy you wanted me to meet?"

"Yeah." Royce introduces us.

I wipe my head. My hand comes back wet. "I'm sorry about that. Something came up."

Tyke rolls down his rear window. He's sitting behind Royce. "I knew you were gonna chicken out."

"He didn't say nothing about that." Royce first looks to Andre, then to me. He moves his shades down a little. "Right?"

"Right, right. I told you, I could use the money." I still want to help the baby—Eva's daughter.

Andre's short-sleeve shirt strains around his biceps like it's a size too small. "He gets one more shot."

Tyke glares at me. "You heard him—one."

"No problem."

"I like to get to know the people trying to be in my crew. Get in," Andre says.

It doesn't sound like I have a choice, so I go with it. "Cool."

I try pulling the back door open where Tyke is sitting.

"You serious? Other side," he says with an attitude.

Inside the car the air conditioner is up high and the leather seats are cold. I can't complain, though. I just let my legs get used to it.

On the visor above Andre is a picture of him and his daughter. I didn't notice before, but she's got his smile, including the gap between his teeth.

The car starts moving and I'm having a hard time with the seat belt. Every time I pull it out, it stops short. Tyke laughs at me. "What? You think he can't drive?" His squeaky voice gets higher with every word. "You don't need that." I let the seat belt slap back into position. I never sat in a car without using one, and it feels wrong not having it on now.

"So, where we dropping you?" Andre asks.

I can't tell them where I'm really going without having to explain why, and there's no way I'm doing that. I think about Royce's cell and that gives me an idea. I tell them I have to pay my mom's cell phone bill—on the same block as the hospital.

"It's late, and if it doesn't get paid today, they'll cut off service and my mom will be pissed. She couldn't survive without her cell."

Andre's driving way faster than he should, and when we hit a speed bump by the school, our heads smack the ceiling. "Whoa," I say.

Andre studies me through the mirror. "Come on, now, you're not afraid of a little turbulence, are you?"

I shake my head, then look out the window.

"So, Lionel, you go to school with Royce?" Andre asks.

Tyke starts to answer. "No, he don't go to that smart—"

"Wasn't talking to you," Andre says.

"No," I say, cutting my eyes at Tyke.

"You ever deliver for anybody before?" Andre asks.

"No."

"So, you ever had any kind of job?"

Uh-oh, another no from me. Doesn't seem like this is going well. I shake my head.

"You ever in trouble with the police before? Like, they still watching you for something?"

The only police I've ever spoken to is Costello and Maggie, but they don't count. "No."

"He'll do," Andre says. "Give him the cell."

Royce props the sunglasses he's wearing on top of his head, then opens the glove box. I spot a small black gun and the phone. The gun shocks me and I jump a little in my seat but I don't let on.

Royce hands me the cell phone without paying any attention to the gun, so he must've known it was in there.

"Keep it on," Andre says. "Royce will call you when he needs you."

The phone's not an expensive one like Royce has, but I don't care.

We make it to the cell phone store in five minutes, but altogether I've been gone for about twenty. I'm relieved and nervous at the same time. Taking the baby is going to be scary and I'm starting to feel jittery. Like there's an electrical current running through me. I wonder what the nurses will do once they realize the baby is gone.

"Okay, you can drop me here," I say when I spot the cell phone store.

Andre pulls the car over and stops. "You good?"

"Yeah, thanks for the ride."

"No." He points to himself, then me. "I mean, we good, right?"

Tyke cuts in. "Dang, you so thick. He wants to make sure you . . ."

It hits me a little late and I can't stand that it took Tyke to make it clear. "I know what he means, all right? Yeah, Andre, we good. I won't let you down."

"Later," Royce says.

Just as I'm about to open my door, a new black Dodge Charger with twenty-two-inch chrome wheels and blacked-out windows pulls up alongside us. They're so close, I can't get out.

The front passenger window slides down. "Yo, Andre," the passenger says. He's a thick-necked dude with cornrows and a thin mustache. "You playing the wrong game, son. I suggest you back off, you know what I'm sayin'?"

"I ain't got to listen to you. The street is free," Andre says.

That's when the window behind the passenger slides down. It's a white guy with eyes so dark and serious they don't even look like they have pupils. He hangs out of the window and points at Andre. His arm is covered in a sleeve of tattoos. There's so many I can't even make them out. They're just a big swirl of different colors. "Ray thinks otherwise," he says, positioning his fingers like a gun and pulling the trigger as they drive away.

"What was that?" I ask.

"Forget those fools," Andre says. "They ain't nobody."

I get out of the car. "Thanks for the ride."

When they're out of sight, I start moving toward the hospital. Those guys in the Charger were pretty scary. Andre might've said they're nobody but I'm thinking they were definitely somebody. Maybe I should start looking for another job. I walk through the revolving doors feeling so nervous I'm having trouble keeping my hands from shaking.

In the lobby the security guard is busy texting. Thankfully he's got a lot to say and doesn't notice me.

In the crowded elevator, a woman holds on to a blue balloon that says IT'S A BOY, while mostly everyone else holds bouquets of flowers. The elevator fills with their scent and makes me think of Miss D. and how she helped to fill that empty lot with flowers. We all get off on the third floor, only they head for the nursery windows, and I head for the little room leading into the nursery where Jasmina had me put on a paper gown. I'm too busy keeping my eyes on Cheryl at the desk down the hall to watch where I'm going. Before I know it, I slam right into someone. It's just like that one time when I walked into a glass door not realizing it was closed. I bounce back a little, first noticing shiny black shoes, then as I look up, a large key ring. It's the security guard who came hurrying over too late when I almost knocked Nelson out.

He looks down at me, and this time he isn't carrying any Hershey bars. "Can I help you?"

I gasp and the words twist in my throat.

His fingers tap his hips while he waits for an answer. "Well?"

The words that finally come are weak even though my head tells them to be strong. I haven't done anything wrong, at least not yet. "No. No, thank you."

"Are you lost?" he asks, pointing to the nursery windows. "If you're here to see a sibling, the windows are that way."

He doesn't remember me. I search the hallway behind him and spot a water fountain. "I know. I was just going to get a drink, thanks." I slowly walk away and hope he's not watching.

After four long gulps of water, I let myself scan the hallway. The guard is gone, and luckily Cheryl is still at the desk, only now there are other nurses with her.

I keep my head turned away from Cheryl and quickly slip inside the little windowless room.

My hands are clammy, so I wipe them on my pants. It doesn't help, though, because a few seconds later I have to do it again. I'm in luck. There's a stack of blue scrubs on the shelf next to the gowns. I put a set on over my clothes. A little big, but they work.

I listen at the door leading into the nursery but it's quiet. I wonder how that can be when the last time I was in here there were at least seven babies squirming around in their little laundry basket cribs.

I put my hand to the doorknob, letting the coolness of it spread to my fingertips. Slowly I turn the knob, but when I push at the door, it doesn't open. I'm about to try again when I remember the key pad on the wall. I don't have a code! I can't believe I forgot about it. The room feels so much smaller now and I'm too hot to think straight.

All of a sudden I'm aware of Cheryl's unmistakable laughter in the hallway.

Think!

After Cheryl quiets down, I hear something very familiar. The squeak of Jasmina's rubber Crocs against the tile floor.

Wait. Jasmina. She mentioned her lucky number. Maybe that's the code she used to get in when I first visited the baby. Only I can't remember what it was.

I try picturing her as she pressed the numbers on the key pad. The beeping sounds—three of them, I think—but her fingers moved too quickly for me to remember.

I start to take the scrubs off when the squeaks stop, but I only manage to get one leg out of the pants before the door leading into the hallway swings open, almost knocking me to the floor.

12

Cheryl stands in the doorway, almost completely blocking it. Her hand flies to her chest when she sees me. Her red velvet cake hair falls in front of her eyes. "Oh!"

"What's wrong?" Jasmina squeezes in next to her, getting a look at me. "Lionel?"

Even though she says my name, it seems as if she's not really sure it's me.

A prickly sensation inches across my scalp like an army of nervous ants. I've only had this happen once before, and that's when Mom caught me going through her coat pockets looking for gum when I was eight.

"What on earth are you doing in here?"

Helping Eva fix her mistake!

I hope Jasmina will at least smile at seeing me but she doesn't. Her face is hard and impossible to read.

My throat is dry. "Oh, hi, I, um . . . um . . ."

Cheryl scans the little room for clues. "Um, what? This room is off limits to visitors."

"Well . . . I . . . I wanted to see the baby."

I can tell Jasmina wants to believe me by the way her light brown eyes soften. Just as I'm about to relax, Cheryl steps farther into the room.

"Something about that just doesn't feel right. You wanted to see the baby without a nurse escort?" Cheryl says. The dryness in my throat makes my voice its prisoner.

Just then, the door with the key pad opens, surprising me. It's an unfamiliar nurse. "Is everything all right in here? I heard yelling." She's got an accent like Anisa's mom. I hadn't even thought about who was in the nursery taking care of the babies.

Cheryl's face is red. It's like her whole top half has gone up in a blazing fire.

"I got this, Lisa, thank you."

Once Lisa goes back inside, Cheryl turns to me. "You look awfully suspicious sweating in those scrubs." She pauses, then, "I have a good mind to call security." *Oh, no!* "Jazzy, do you believe this?" she says after a few seconds. "I don't even think he's listening."

It's been too long since I left Anisa. I think about Mr. Owen and Miss D. and wonder if there's a chance they're not too worried about me. Maybe Mom will blame them for not keeping a closer eye on me. They're the last people who should get into trouble because of something I did. But more than anything, I hope Eva is okay.

"Please, don't . . . ," I manage. "I just wanted to see the baby."

Finally Jasmina says, "Cheryl, I don't think calling security will be necessary. I'd like to handle this, if I may?"

My shoulders sag with relief but I'm not safe yet. Cheryl takes her time deciding my fate. Her frosty blue eyes grow squinty until I think maybe she's trying to make me disappear.

At last she says, "Okay. *But,* I had better not see you around here again, do you understand?"

For the first time since getting caught, I'm able to take a deep breath. It feels good, like all along I've been trying to breathe in a space with hardly any air. "Yes, ma'am."

She points to the scrubs I'm half wearing. "Take them off and put them into the garbage."

Jasmina doesn't say a word to me as I follow her to her office, but that changes once we're inside.

She sits at her desk, then motions for me to take the seat across from her, but I only sit on the edge, ready to bolt if I have to. "Okay, Lionel, you'd better start talking and quickly."

Her voice is cold and I don't like the way she's staring at me like I'm a stranger.

Anisa was right—this was a stupid idea. Probably the stupidest thing I've ever tried to do. If Jasmina hadn't spoken up when she did, I might've ended up in a police car again. Only this time I would've deserved to be there.

I keep my eyes on my beat-up old sneakers because I'm

afraid Jasmina will be able to see the whole truth in my face. "I told you. I just wanted to see the baby, that's all. And when I came to your office, I saw that you were busy and didn't want to bother you."

"Lionel, please look at me," she says.

I do what she asks.

"I like you, and honestly, I think you're a good kid." She points to her spiky white hair. "As you can tell from these, I've been at this a very long time and I have to agree with Cheryl. Something—I don't know what it is—doesn't feel right."

For a minute I think about how good it'd feel to tell Jasmina everything, because all of a sudden, I'm exhausted. Maybe she'll give the baby back to Eva for a second chance like the one she just gave me. I know Eva would want that.

After all, Eva didn't mean to leave the baby. I just know it. All I'd have to do is part my lips and the words will come spilling out like water from a broken faucet.

But I can't. I just can't betray Eva like that.

It's not like Jasmina has asked me a question exactly, so I bite my top lip to make sure I stay quiet.

"I can't force you to tell me what's going on, Lionel," Jasmina says. "But I can tell you that I'm here for you if you need me. And I mean for anything." She pauses before adding, "You also mentioned your dad the other day, so maybe I can help with that too."

"My father? What's he got to do with this?"

Jasmina leans back in her chair, getting comfortable like we're going to be here awhile. I'm thankful she got Cheryl to let me go, but it's after five. I should've been out of here already.

"Well, your mom told me a little bit, but right now I'm thinking of something you said. It was about how fathers never care about anybody but themselves. Do you really feel that way, Lionel?"

My stomach flip-flops the way it does when the teacher calls on me and I don't have the answer. I need to get back to Anisa and Eva, not sit here wasting time talking about my father. "Yes." I pause, hoping she's satisfied. Then I ask, "Am I in trouble, or can I go now?"

Jasmina acts like I haven't asked her anything.

"You know, when a parent leaves a child, it's because they have issues. Ones they need to work out for themselves that have absolutely nothing to do with the child."

I don't want to talk about this even if it's the truth. I have to go.

"Lionel, there is no cure for feeling as you probably do, deserted . . ."

I wish there was. "By your father. Those feelings are . . ."

Sucky, that's what they are.

". . . pretty intense and can be hard to sort out," she continues. "But you don't have to do it all on your own. You have your mom—"

"BUT I NEED HIM TOO."

The power of my voice bounces off the walls of the tiny office, but Jasmina doesn't even move.

My throat is closing again but I manage to force my words through anyway. "And he doesn't even care! I'm nothing to him."

Jasmina takes my hand across the desk. I expect her fingers to be soft and delicate but they're not. They're strong and full of purpose like maybe she's trying to give me some of her strength. My own fingers unexpectedly curl themselves around hers.

"Sweetheart, what you are is a good and brave young man. Whatever is going on in your father's head are his problems to work out. Not yours. Not now, not ever. He is missing out on knowing you, Lionel."

I tighten my grip, as if that'll make her words true.

We sit that way for a while longer, and before I get up to leave, I ask, "What if the baby's mother changed her mind? What if she wants her back?"

"If any of those things happened, it would be up to a judge to decide whether to press criminal charges."

Jasmina's not making any sense. Eva's not a criminal. "Charges? You mean the mother could go to jail?"

"It really depends on the judge and the circumstances. Why do you ask?"

"Just wondering," I say, hoping I haven't said too much.

"You shouldn't worry about any of that, Lionel. You're a hero in all of this."

Jasmina's bright smile does nothing to make me feel better. Eva might go to jail and I have no idea what I'm supposed to do now.

I head out of the hospital full of worry. I can't imagine Eva going to jail because she made one mistake. It's not like she goes around doing dumb things all the time. Maybe the judge will see that and go easy on her. Maybe he'll make her take lessons on how to be a good mother. Or maybe Eva could promise to do some kind of volunteer work for the rest of her life if she has to.

"Hey," I hear when I get a few blocks away from the hospital. "Don't losers have *anything* to do?" It's Tyke. He's got his head out the back window of Andre's parked car. Royce is sitting next to him. A guy from Andre's crew sits in the front passenger seat.

Royce is on his cell but hangs up. "Man, Tyke, don't you see he doesn't feel like talking to you? Leave him alone."

"So what, I'm talking to him. Yo, I asked you a question!"

Tyke is on me constantly and I'm really tired of him. Before I know what I'm doing, I get closer to the car, then reach in and grab Tyke's shirt. "Shut up!" I scream into his face.

Andre whips around toward me from the front seat. He's got a beer bottle between his knees. "Yo, what's your problem, Lionel?" He sounds as angry as he did on the basketball court.

"It's all right," Tyke says. "I got this." He jumps out of the car.

"Hold up, leave him alone," Royce says.

I take my eyes off Tyke to look at Royce and that's when a white light flashes and I hit the ground hard.

Tyke hit me just below my eye. The pain is fierce.

"Keep your hands off me," Tyke says.

"Why'd you do that?" Royce says, getting out of the car. "You didn't have to hit him."

Two women carrying grocery bags across the street yell for us to break it up and go home.

Royce holds his hand out to me but I wave him off and get up on my own. Just then we spot the Dodge Charger that pulled up earlier driving toward us again. This time all of their windows are open.

"Oh, no," Royce says.

When a policeman from down the block sees the commotion and starts to make his way over, the Charger flips a U-turn and drives off.

"That was a stupid move, Tyke. Let's go!" Andre says.

Both Royce and Tyke scramble back inside the car, and then they're gone.

The policeman is tall and black and looks like he could bench-press two of me if he wanted. He reaches me in no time. His bald head is shiny with sweat. "What's going on?"

My face hurts and my hands sting from hitting the ground, but I think I'm okay. "Nothing, nothing."

A boy younger than me walks by with earphones in. He

stares at us as he crosses the street like maybe something bad is about to go down.

"You know those guys?" the police officer says.

"Yeah."

"Why were you two fighting?"

"He just doesn't like me, I guess."

"Hmmm . . . really?"

I nod, probably too quickly, because now my head hurts.

He looks me in the eye. "You feeling all right? Any dizziness or anything?"

I shake my head, slowly.

"Are you afraid? Do you want me to walk you home?"

"No, that's okay." I back up. "But thank you anyway."

On the way home, I catch my reflection in a bank window. My eye has already begun to swell. There's even a little purplish color starting to show. I feel all kinds of stupid for letting Tyke, as small as he is, sucker-punch me. I'm having a terrible week and it's only Tuesday.

I'll have to cover up my throbbing eye with Mom's makeup before she gets home. But it'll have to wait until after checking on Eva and telling Anisa I've failed.

Finally I make it to the busy courtyard. Some of the little kids are riding their bikes in figure eights, totally oblivious, and I'm jealous. I don't want to know what I know. I especially don't want to tell Anisa about the possibility of Eva going to jail.

Mr. Owen's crew is playing dominoes at their small folding table. I put my hand to the side of my face as I pass. I don't want to be seen by anyone. I also don't want to be asked a bunch of questions about my black eye.

I almost make it by unnoticed but Mr. Santiago must have some kind of radar. "Hey, Lionel, where you been?"

Without turning around I answer, "Oh, I had to . . . um . . . help Anisa."

"Well, you got Mr. Owen looking for you."

That's the least of my problems now. "You didn't happen to see Anisa's mom," I ask, making sure not to give them a full view of my face, "did you, Mr. Santiago?"

"No, not since this morning."

Just then Mr. Brown stands and stretches out his long string bean legs. "I've got to catch the six o'clock bus up to Carroll Gardens. Need to help Retta with her dinner. She likes giving the nursing staff a hard way to go when supper comes around."

"You tell Loretta I'm waiting on her to get back and make me some of her greens. Nobody can do them up like she does, and that includes the head cook. You'd think the navy would train them better but they don't. Just last night, he cooked them to death."

"You feeling okay, Santiago?" Mr. Brown asks.

"Yeah, just fine. Now don't forget to tell Loretta what I said, hear?"

"Will do. I'll catch y'all later."

I take that as my cue and continue toward my building.

Inside, Mr. Owen is about to step into the elevator. I almost duck back onto the stoop but he catches me.

He lets the elevator door close. "Lionel, where have you been? I was just about to knock on Anisa's door looking for you."

I don't look at him fully. "I'm sorry, I had to help Anisa with something." It's not a lie, not really. "It just took a lot longer than I thought it would."

"Well, you got Miss D. all upset over you. And please look at me when I'm talking to you."

I can't hide my eye any longer, and when I look at him, I see he's got sweat stains the size of pancakes underneath his arms. "So, you fighting now?" he says, coming closer to get a better look at my eye.

I've never had a real fight in my whole life including what happened with Nelson. I don't think what happened with Tyke could officially be called one either. I never saw it coming. Maybe that's something my father was supposed to teach me. To be prepared for anything so I don't become somebody's punching bag. And what makes it even worse is it was somebody smaller than me. I should've been able to take Tyke.

"No, it wasn't a fight."

"Really?" he says. "That only leaves walking into a door or getting beat up. Which one was it?"

I need something to drink because my voice comes out sounding like somebody scraped a chair across the floor. "The door one."

Mr. Owen lets out half of a laugh. "How did I know you were going to say that?"

I shrug, embarrassed.

"If your new friends happened to have something to do with you *walking* into the door, maybe you should rethink your friends."

"They didn't," I lie.

"Come on upstairs with me. I can . . ."

"No!" I snap without thinking, because the only place I need to go is back to Anisa's apartment.

Mr. Owen looks hurt and it doesn't take me long to wish I could take it back. ". . . help you with that eye," he finishes.

My eye can wait. "I'm sorry, I didn't mean it. But no, thanks. I'll take care of it."

"I can help you with a whole lot of stuff if you'll allow me. Will you?"

Mr. Owen waits patiently for an answer. I study the creases in his dark brown face, trying to decide. Letting him help me will make my life easier but maybe Eva's life worse. But I only had one plan for taking the baby and now I don't have any. Mr. Owen puts his arm across my shoulders and I let him lead me onto the elevator. I haven't decided to tell him, I just need to chill for a little while.

• • •

The first thing Mr. Owen does is turn the living room window fan on high, then he calls Miss D. to let her know I'm okay. He tells me he doesn't want her seeing my eye just yet.

A pen and today's newspaper sit on the coffee table. The paper is opened to the crossword puzzle. It starts flapping around in the wind as soon as the fan builds up speed.

"Have a seat on the couch. I'll be right back."

If what Mr. Owen has planned for my eye doesn't work, I'll go back to plan A and use the makeup. I don't know what Mom will do if she finds out what happened. She might even go around to where Tyke lives to tell his mother what he did. If she does that, there will be no living it down.

Mr. Owen is still in the bathroom. I don't know what could be taking him so long.

A few more newspaper pages stir in the wind and the words "Baby Doe" catch my eye. I put the paper on my lap and find the article. It's about Eva's baby. My skin tingles all over and my chest burns like I've been running.

I'm afraid of how much of what really happened will be in the article. Still, I take a deep breath and begin to read.

13

Police Search for the Mother of Baby Doe

A baby girl was discovered by two teenagers at a construction site on Sunday afternoon. Though it's unclear why they were there, some are calling it a case of divine intervention. At the time of discovery, the baby was weak and had spent several hours alone. Without the discovery, Baby Doe most likely would have died from dehydration.

Although New York State introduced the Safe Haven law in July of 2000, there are still quite a number of unwanted babies abandoned in New York City each year.

The Safe Haven law allows a parent to leave a newborn anonymously without being criminally charged as long as the newborn is abandoned in a safe environment such as a firehouse, hospital, or police station.

Brooklyn Councilwoman Julia Lugo had this to

say to the New York *Daily News*: "The number of abandoned babies continues to grow, proving that the public needs to be re-educated about the Safe Haven law and how it works. As of today, I'm making it my duty to ensure every mother in this borough is aware of her options. With that said, I am announcing a new campaign that will take on this very important task. It will include bus and subway signs as well as an updated website. I am determined to get the word out."

I read the article again and again. We're going to need somebody on Eva's side, so I scribble the name Julia Lugo down on the palm of my hand. I'm not sure she'll help us but it's worth trying.

Just as I stand to leave, Mr. Owen puts a cotton ball and a clear medicine bottle on the table in front of me. "Sorry for taking so long," he says. "Had trouble finding the castor oil."

"Oh, that's okay."

He motions toward the newspaper. "Anything interesting?"

"Um, yeah," I say, placing the paper on the table. "It's about the baby we found." I inch closer to the door. "You know something? My eye doesn't hurt so much," I lie. "I'm just going to go home and put some ice on it."

Mr. Owen sits on the couch. "Oh, no, you're not. You come right back here and let me take care of it."

Another few inches and I'm at the door. All I'd have to

do is turn the knob, yank the door open, and I'd be gone. I could be down at least one whole staircase by the time Mr. Owen steps one foot out of the door. Maybe he won't even come after me.

With my hand clutching the knob I say, "No, thank you. I . . ."

His voice is so strong and clear, it surprises me. "Lionel, I might've been born at night but it surely was not last night. What are you up to?"

My body goes warm all at once, with my ears burning the hottest. "Nothing, I just want to go home."

He hops to his feet. "Get over here."

Mr. Owen sounds like he means business, so I drag myself back to the couch. "Sit," he orders. "What's going on?"

"I just read an article about the baby we found and it kind of upset me, that's all."

Mr. Owen reads the article. "I think Ms. Lugo's idea is a smart one. There are still lots of folks out there who have never heard of the Safe Haven law. A lack of knowledge doesn't make someone, I don't know, a kind of heathen."

"Somebody called me that. What does it mean?"

He looks at me strangely and I'm sorry I brought it up. "Who called you that?"

I lean back. "Anisa's mother."

With a long noisy groan, Mr. Owen takes off his baseball cap, then flips it onto the table. There's an indent in his white curly hair that goes all the way around his head. "Anisa's mother shouldn't go around calling children names, period. It's not right."

He pours the liquid from the bottle onto the cotton ball. "Don't worry, it won't hurt. It'll just help with the swelling."

I talk while he dabs my throbbing eye. "So, what does it mean?"

"Somebody who doesn't believe in God."

"Well, I don't go to church . . ."

"That doesn't mean a thing, Lionel. Four walls don't matter to God. All that matters is what's in there," he says, pointing to my chest. "Trust me on that."

And I do, but I'm too afraid to trust anybody with what I know about Eva.

Mr. Owen goes into the kitchen and comes out with a giant bag of frozen peas. "A ghetto ice pack for your eye." He laughs, handing it to me. The bag is more than cold and I can barely stand it against my skin.

"Your mom told me a little bit about your father. How long has it been since you've seen him?" he asks.

This is major none-of-anybody's-business stuff. I shrug the question off. "Six years?"

I don't want to talk about my father. I turn the bag around, then place it over both eyes, hoping Mr. Owen will take the hint. But he doesn't notice. He just goes right on blabbing.

"In a way, I guess you've been abandoned too, huh?"

My head starts pounding and I push the bag tighter against my hurting eye. I don't want to cry in front of Mr. Owen but I'm not sure I can stop it. It's like something is pulling me in different directions. I still love my father, and at the same time, I hate him.

"It could happen at any age. Look at how Miss Dorothy's son abandoned her and she's O-L-D."

The way he spells out "old" makes me laugh. A little. Just my lips blowing out some air, not a big ha-ha or anything. That's when he puts his hand on my knee and squeezes it.

Then Mr. Owen gets serious. "Do you remember when I said you don't have any control over what somebody else does, only what you do? How you respond?"

I nod.

"Well, I wanted to tell you how I put that to use after my son left."

"How?" I ask, moving the ice pack a little so I can see Mr. Owen's softened face. He's looking at me but I'm not really sure he's seeing me. He seems to be lost in his thoughts.

He closes up the bottle of castor oil, then says, "I responded by writing him a letter telling him everything I've ever felt about him, from the day he was born until the day he left. I didn't hold anything back. I also let him know I'd always welcome him with open arms if he ever found his way back to me."

"What did he do when he got the letter?"

"I couldn't send it because I had no idea where he went. It's been sitting inside my night table waiting on an address since the day after he left."

"So why did you even write it if you couldn't mail it?"

"Because it felt good to respond to him leaving. Getting it all down on paper was better than not saying it at all."

We're quiet for the rest of the time, and it's not weird or anything, like when you're usually around an adult with nothing to say. With him, it's just comfortable, and now I wish I could stay here, but I know I can't.

My face is numb from the bag of peas by the time I leave. I can't feel my cheeks when I thank Mr. Owen for his help or when I ask him not to tell Mom about my eye because I want to be the one to do it. The only thing is, I'm lying.

Mr. Owen walks me to my apartment door and waits until I'm inside before leaving. I watch him through the peephole until he's out of sight. I count to fifty, then sneak down to Anisa's.

Nervously, I knock on the door, wondering what I'm about to walk into.

It seems like forever before Anisa finally appears. Her long dark ponytail looks like the mane of a horse—messy and fanned across her shoulder. Her eyes are bloodshot and worried and her face is shiny with sweat.

First she searches the hallway behind me, then drags me inside, locking the door.

Anisa's voice is a sharp whisper. "What happened?" I start to answer but she doesn't give me a chance. "Did you get her? Where is she?"

"No, I didn't get her. I'm sorry . . . I got caught."

She gently touches the side of my face. "Did they do that to your eye?"

I'm too embarrassed to even tell Anisa how I let Tyke punch me. "No, I walked into a door. Jasmina talked a nurse into not turning me in. How's Eva?"

Anisa's eyes shine hopefully. "She's not bleeding anymore. That's good, right?"

"Yeah, but what about the fever?"

"She still has it. I've tried talking Eva into going to the hospital, but she won't go. And she made me swear on my Bible that I won't call my mother." Anisa starts to cry. "What are we going to do?"

I wrap my arms around her. I don't think about it, I just do it. Anisa is always so strong, and to feel her trembling now brings out something new in me. I want—no, need—to protect and comfort her.

"Don't worry, Anisa." I pull back so that I can see her face. Then I tell her about the newspaper article and the things Julia Lugo said about the Safe Haven law.

I show her the name written in the palm of my hand. "Julia will help us. And I'll be here with you no matter what happens. You won't have to do anything alone."

"Okay," Anisa says quietly.

In the kitchen, I dial information for Julia Lugo's phone number. When I call, her voice mail answers. I think about hanging up, but only for a second.

"Hi, we have important information about the baby who was found at the construction site. Please call us back—but," I quickly add, "it has to be soon. Really soon, or . . . we won't be here." I leave the number of the cell Royce gave me.

Anisa goes in to check on Eva while we wait. "She's asleep," she says when she comes back.

We sit quietly on the edge of the couch. I hold on to the cell, willing it to ring, but instead, Anisa's house phone rings, scaring us to death.

I follow Anisa back into the kitchen. Anisa catches it on the third ring, taking a deep breath before answering.

"Hello?"

I watch her face closely, trying to figure out who it is.

Anisa's voice slips into cheerful mode. It's a big difference from just a couple of minutes ago and it makes me upset to think that it might be a long time before she'll be cheerful for real.

"Okay, Mami. Take your time and don't worry about us. We'll just heat something up for dinner."

I close my eyes and lean against the washing machine tucked into the space between the kitchen sink and the cabinets, waiting for Anisa to get off the phone. Since all the apartments in the projects have the same size kitchen, everyone who has a machine keeps it in the exact same spot. Sometimes my mother folds a towel on top of ours and uses it to iron clothes on. When Miss D. isn't using hers, she keeps a tablecloth and a vase full of fake roses on top. There's only a laundry basket filled with clean clothes on Anisa's. I don't even notice when Anisa hangs up, and when I open my eyes, I'm shocked to see her standing next to me. She puts her arms around my waist, resting her head against my chest. It's strange for sure but nice all the same.

"My mom is eating dinner at my aunt's house. She'll be home later."

I don't want to, but after a couple of minutes I tell her that I have to get up to my apartment and that I'll come back after dinner. "If Julia calls, I'll tell her we need help fast. When your mom finds out, we're going to need her on our side, because . . ."

"There's no doubt my mom is going to go completely crazy."

I nod, hoping I'll make it back before Mrs. Torres gets home.

14

In Mom's makeup drawer, I find a small tube of something that says "cover-up." It's exactly what I need.

Mom's skin is a little lighter than mine, so it isn't going to match me exactly, but I have to take my chances. There's more important stuff for me to worry about.

The bathroom is brighter, so I use the mirror in there.

There's a small puffy purple spot underneath my eye. It hurts to rub the makeup in, but I keep adding more. I look like I have a birthmark on my face when I'm done, so I add a little brown eye shadow too.

Mom should be walking through the door any minute. I check my face three different times from every angle. It doesn't look good at all. For one, the brown eye shadow has tiny sparkles in it, and two, there's a spot of blood on the white of my eye. There's no way to hide that. I might as well draw an arrow on my cheek pointing to it.

My palms are sweaty and make Julia's phone number almost unreadable. I copy it onto a piece of paper, then slip it into my pocket. I scrub my hands until all of the ink is gone.

In my bedroom, I check the time and then the window for Mom. I only watch for about two minutes before I spot her making her way through our courtyard. She stops to talk to Mr. Santiago and I wish she'd hurry up. Waiting to find out my fate has never been easy.

Finally, she walks into our building.

The door to our apartment opens. A couple seconds later, "Lionel?"

I dig out a baseball cap from my closet and put it on, keeping the brim low. It helps, but not much. Maybe if I confess up front she'll take it easier on me. I mean, being honest has to be worth something.

"I'm in my room, Mom."

"Come help me start dinner, please."

I glance in the mirror before leaving the safety of my room. I'm doomed. My face is a swirl of colors—and the sparkles from the makeup definitely don't help. If this goes down bad, I doubt Mom will let me go anywhere. If I'm lucky, she'll buy the door story.

She calls again. "Did you hear me?"

I adjust the hat so the brim blocks my face a little more. "I'll be right there," I say, remembering to put my cell on vibrate.

Mom is at the kitchen sink washing some lettuce. Her heels are by the door. I don't remember the last time she bought herself a new pair of shoes. These are starting to look worn down with a big scrape on the toe. She keeps polishing them, though, trying to keep them as nice as she can.

Standing in her stocking feet, she asks, "How was your day?"

She's not looking at me, so I make myself busy setting the table. "Fine."

"How did Miss Dorothy's go?" she asks, slicing a tomato with a knife.

"Pretty good. Mr. Owen was there too. I helped him do some stuff for Miss D."

"So the piano lesson went well?"

She puts the knife down noisily, and just as I'm about to answer, she says, "Why are you wearing your hat in the house? You know I don't like that. Please take it off."

"But *I* like it." As soon as it's out of my mouth, I know it was a mistake.

She pokes my shoulder. "Please turn around, Lionel."

I do what I'm told but keep my good side toward her. She takes hold of my chin and turns my head.

"What happened?"

I look at her full-on for the first time and flinch when she angrily snatches the hat off my head.

"Didn't I ask you a question?" Her words are hard and as stiff as her starched work shirt.

"I walked into the bathroom door."

"Am I supposed to believe that?"

I'm not sure if I should answer. I look down at her toes.

They're polished almost the same shade of red as the blood staining my eye.

She asks a second time.

"Somebody accidentally hit me. It's not like I was fighting or anything."

"An accident, huh? Did this *accident* have anything to do with Royce or Tyke when you left the building?"

So that's what she and Mr. Santiago were talking about all that time. I don't answer. I don't even nod.

"Because," she continues, "I seem to remember telling you not to leave the building. Do you remember that, Lionel?"

I keep my mouth tightly closed. It's not easy with her asking questions I'm not even sure she wants me to answer.

Her head moves as she speaks and her dark curls jiggle. "I'm working at the bank, taking all kinds of nastiness from rude customers, just so you can have a decent life, and you're out there fighting in the street and acting like a common thug?"

I wasn't acting like anything but I won't tell her that. I won't say anything. The less I say, the better off I'll be and the quicker I'll be able to get back to Anisa.

"Is that how it's going to be from now on?"

I'm only trying to do what's right.

"Is that what you want? To be nothing but a thug in life?"

She's making me angry but I have to keep quiet.

"Lionel, I'm talking to you!" *Keep quiet.*

Mom pulls my arm. "Answer me!"

My plan crumbles like a sand castle smashed by a wave. "GOD, MOM! WHAT'S WRONG WITH YOU? I TOLD YOU I WASN'T FIGHTING!" The yelling makes my eye feel like it might pop out of my head.

Mom slaps me across the face, but it's her eyes that fill with tears, not mine. Her hand leaves a million bee stings on my cheek. "Don't you ever raise your voice to me again! You think you grown and can say what you like and do as you please?" She gets closer to me. "I'm here to tell you that won't be happening, Lionel. From now on, after you leave Miss Dorothy's, Mr. Owen will be walking you back here like you're some kind of baby, because you're not to be trusted, just like your father."

It's almost like she's slapped me again. Her hands fly to her mouth as if she's trying to push those last words back inside, but it's too late.

There's no way I'd ever think about not being there for Anisa, Eva, and the baby. Not ever. That's something my father would do, not me. "I'm nothing like him and I never will be."

She wipes her eyes, then reaches for me. "I didn't mean that, Lionel. It's just . . . I want more for you, and sometimes I'm afraid."

I let her hug me but I don't return it. She hasn't even asked if my eye hurts or if I'm okay.

We finish getting everything ready and when we sit down to dinner it's quicker than usual because I don't have an appetite. The silence is thick and loud, and all I can think of is getting back to Anisa. I'm already washing my dish by the time Mom is done eating.

"Can I go talk to Anisa for a little while?" I ask.

She hesitates and for a minute I think she might say no, but then she says, "Okay, but not for long. And don't leave the building."

Just as I walk out, she tells me she loves me, but I pretend not to hear her.

I listen at Anisa's door for a couple of minutes before knocking. Anisa opens the door right away. Her quick smile gives me a tiny bit of happiness.

As soon as I step inside, though, reality takes over. Except for the ticking of the kitchen clock, the apartment is quiet. The setting sun shines through the window blinds. Dust particles drift around the living room like we're standing inside a snow globe.

"How's Eva?"

Anisa's cheeks and neck are splotched red with worry. "I think she's okay. She's still asleep. Any word from Julia?"

"No, and it's almost seven thirty."

"Maybe we should call again," Anisa says. "People work late all the time."

She's right, so I dial from my cell. It rings three times before someone picks up. At first I think it might be the machine again, but it's not.

"Julia Lugo speaking."

"Hello?" I say quickly.

Without warning, Anisa tries to grab the phone from me. I almost drop it. "Maybe we shouldn't! Hang up," she says.

"No, stop. We have to," I say quickly, moving out of Anisa's reach. "Yes, hello?"

The voice on the phone sounds rushed. She's probably sorry she even answered. "This is Julia Lugo; how may I help you?"

It's hard to keep my voice from shaking. I hope Eva can forgive me for telling on her, but I—*we*—have to. "I know who left the baby at the construction site. Can you help us?"

It feels so good to finally be able to say these words to someone who can do something. I take a big breath and let it out slowly.

Anisa reaches for me, and I think she might try taking the phone away again, but she only wants to hold my hand.

"Yes, yes, I can absolutely help you. Is the mother with you now and is she okay?"

"She's with us but we don't think she's okay. She's bleeding a lot and has a fever."

There's noise on the other end like maybe Julia's moving papers around. "Okay, she needs medical attention immediately. Give me your name and address and I'll get an ambulance over to you."

I give Julia the information she needs.

"Lionel, you sound young. How old are you?"

"I'm thirteen."

"Well, I want you to know you're doing the right thing. I'll meet you at the hospital."

After I hang up I break the news to Anisa that Julia is sending an ambulance for Eva. She doubles over and sobs. I have to fight hard to keep from doing the same. It's up to me to be strong, though. To be here for Anisa, because she needs me more than anyone's ever needed me.

It's not easy to put Anisa's mother out of my mind but I have to. All that matters right now is Anisa and getting help for Eva.

I try calming her down the best I can. "Listen, it'll be okay. Julia's going to meet us at the hospital."

But Anisa's not listening and now she's trembling again. I take her in my arms and hold her tightly.

"They'll be here soon," I whisper, "so we should wake Eva up. Maybe put some of her things into a bag to take to the hospital, okay?"

She steps back and looks at me. Her nose is stuffed from crying and her voice sounds like she has a cold. "You don't understand, Lionel. You don't know how mad my mother's going to be."

I think about how Anisa's mother looked that day in Jasmina's tiny office at the hospital. There's no denying how crazy she might get, but I know we're doing the right thing. Julia confirmed it. I won't think about anything else and I won't let Anisa either.

"Put that out of your head. You're helping your sister, that's it." She seems to hear me. "Okay, let's go wake her up."

In the bedroom, I gently shake Eva's shoulder while Anisa fills a small bag with the things she might need.

But Eva doesn't budge, not even with all the noise Anisa's making, and that scares me. Without letting Anisa see, I place a shaky hand on her back to make sure she's breathing. It rises and falls, and I sigh with relief.

I nudge again. "Come on, Eva. You have to—"

Just then there's a loud knock on the door.

Anisa drops the bag and freezes. "They're here."

I force my unsteady legs to take me to the door. Anisa follows.

Before we get the chance to open it, the hurried voice of Anisa's mother fills the hallway. Even though her English is broken, it's easy to understand her.

"Why're you here? Nobody called you. Go away, *ahora*! Now!"

Anisa cries quietly. "Lionel, I can't do this. I can't."

I start thinking crazy, weighing just how hurt I'd get if I jumped out of the window. It's only the second floor; maybe it wouldn't be so bad. But then I think about Mr. Owen's words again. How you'd be surprised by what you're capable of doing when it comes down to the nitty-gritty. This has to be my nitty-gritty—maybe Anisa's too.

I weave my arm through Anisa's, getting as close to her

as I can. I picture us being a wall or a dam getting ready to hold back the forces of a tidal wave.

When the door swings open, Anisa's mother gasps at the sight of us, then spits out words to Anisa in Spanish. Her cold green eyes zero in on me as she speaks, but I don't let them spook me. The paramedics, two women, wait behind her.

We weren't standing as close as I'd thought because Anisa presses even closer to me. Her voice is small and weak. "Lionel was only helping. Eva needs help, Mami. She's sick and there was . . . blood."

"*Sangre!* Blood! Evalisse?" Anisa's mother makes her way toward Eva's room but Eva stumbles out first.

Poor Bella, crying and scared, tries to run to her mom, but Anisa scoops her up first.

"Don't worry, Mami, I'm . . ." Eva tries but then her eyes roll back, showing only the whites. She falls to the floor and the paramedics rush to her.

15

take the steps two at a time. When I get to my floor, Mom is already in the hallway. She's changed out of her work clothes and into sweatpants and a top. "What's happening, Lionel? Are you okay?"

I'm out of breath and I've got the worst stomachache of my life. "I'm okay, Mom. But something happened to Eva." My voice breaks and I strain to get the rest of the words out. "Something bad."

Mom frowns. "What happened? Is she okay?"

"I don't know if she'll be okay."

The next part is hard to say out loud. "Mom, the baby we found is hers."

Her eyes widen. "What?"

We rush down to Anisa's apartment just as Eva is being wheeled out of the building on a stretcher. *"Ay Dios mío,"* Oh, my God, Anisa's mother says over and over.

Everyone is crying, including Bella. Anisa holds Eva's hand and when she looks at me I feel like my heart is splitting in two. Her eyelids are swollen from crying and her face, neck, and arms are red. "It'll be okay," I say, hoping I'm telling the truth.

Me and Mom watch from the stoop as the paramedics load Eva into the ambulance. The rest of the neighborhood watches from the courtyard or their windows.

Once back in our apartment, we sit at the kitchen table, and with my head in my heads, I tell Mom everything. Even the dumb idea I had about trying to steal the baby. I thought maybe she'd freak out on me for that, but she doesn't. She just goes on rubbing my back.

The only things I keep to myself are the job with Royce I'm supposed to be starting and the cell in my front pocket that has just started to vibrate against my thigh. Mom would definitely freak out about that.

I excuse myself and go into the bathroom. I got a voice mail from Royce and he doesn't sound too happy.

"Lionel, it's me. Are you kidding? Why you not answering? You want this job or not?"

I shut the cell off, then slip it back into my pocket. I don't think about Royce for the rest of the night.

For three days, Mom keeps me close and I don't see anybody but Miss D. and Mr. Owen. I try calling Anisa about a million times, but no one answers.

When Miss D. first saw my black eye, and I told the truth about who did it, she took extra good care of me by making a fresh batch of blueberry muffins, and she even let me skip my lesson for that day. Mr. Owen joked that if I kept getting black eyes he'd have to teach me how to box. He put his fists up.

"First things first," he said, hopping from one foot to the other. "The one-two combo. Tyke will never see it coming."

I wasn't in the mood to joke about how I let Tyke punch me, but the more Mr. Owen hopped around in his Nikes, long white socks, and plaid shorts, the more I wanted to laugh.

"Lionel," Miss D. said, "please don't pay any attention to him. Fighting has never solved anything."

Mr. Owen put his hands down, then winked at me. "When she's right, she's right. The bigger man always takes the nonviolent way out. And in this case, you're the bigger man, no pun intended."

So far there had been enough trouble in the past week to last for two summers.

Miss D. pulled me into a tight hug then. Her perfume was kind of spicy but smelled good. "Yes, not only are you bigger, but you're a hero two times over. Not everyone would've done what you did to help Evalisse."

Mr. Owen gave me a long look, then said, "She's right again."

That made me proud and I decided not to think about pounding Tyke into the ground.

• • •

Finally it's Saturday, and I wake to the smell of French toast and bacon, and Mom sitting quietly, wearing her glasses and sipping coffee at the kitchen table. Even Lionel Richie is silent.

She tightens the worn-out belt of her robe. It's old with shredded cuffs and collar, but she says time is what made the material so soft. She'll never throw that thing away. She only wears it when she plans on staying inside all day, though, and seeing that it looks like it's going to rain, I guess that's just what she plans on doing.

"I went down to Anisa's this morning to see if everything's okay." She stares into my eyes, but no matter how hard I try, I can't guess what she's thinking. I sit across from her.

"I don't know how I was ever friends with Maria. She had the nerve to insult how I'm dressed. Can you believe that?"

I almost laugh out loud. Looking at the strings hanging from a hole in her collar, I can definitely believe it. Plus, Anisa's mom just says what she wants when she wants.

"I mean, I swallow my pride and go down there out of concern for her and her girls, and she insults me?" She gives a small laugh. "She did soften the blow with a cup of coffee and I have to admit, I miss her Café Bustelo. Nobody makes it as good as she does."

I don't care about the coffee. "So they're home now?"

"Anisa and Bella were staying with their aunt Doris, in Queens, but they'll be home later today."

I'm afraid to ask but I have to know. "Mom, what about Eva?"

"She's recovering at the hospital from an infection, and by the sound of it, she's lucky her mother didn't disown her. If it wasn't for the councilwoman, Julia Lugo, she might have. But she was able to calm her down and get them some help. There's going to be an investigation and Eva will have to go to court." She takes another long sip from her mug while the words "investigation" and "court" send a horde of goose bumps to my arms and legs.

"Ms. Lugo, though," she finally says, "thinks Eva will be treated with compassion and most likely won't have to serve jail time. She'll definitely have to take parenting classes for at least two years."

The goose bumps retreat right away. "So that means she's getting the baby back, right? Right?"

"Yes, Lionel." Mom smiles. "That's exactly what it means."

I'm so happy, I give Mom a big hug.

Just then the phone rings. Mom picks up the cordless phone but it's dead, so she goes into the living room to get it.

"Lionel, it's for you," she says.

Oh, no, Royce must've gotten my phone number somehow. Mom won't be too happy about him calling me. But when I enter the living room and she hands me the phone, she's got a big smile on her face, and I think I know why.

I take the phone from her. "Anisa?"

"Yeah, it's me!"

"Man, I've been calling you for days. Are you okay?"

"I'm sorry, everything has been really chaotic, but I'm fine."

"That's okay. So, when is the baby coming home?" I sit cross-legged on the living room floor.

"She's with Children's Services right now, but Mom says she'll be home soon. Can you believe it? I'm so happy."

"Me too!"

"And by the way, Eva named the baby Angelina."

The perfect name, in my book.

"You know," Anisa continues more seriously, "if it wasn't for you, Lionel, I don't know what would've happened to my family. Thank you so much."

I smile, relieved to know I made the right decision in calling Julia.

After we hang up, I feel like eating a hundred pieces of French toast and a pound of bacon.

Mom's more than happy to make me a plate.

After I eat breakfast, I get dressed, remembering to stuff the cell phone into my pocket. If Mom found it, she'd flip. Today, I have to help Mr. Owen paint Miss D.'s bedroom. Yesterday, after a not-so-bad piano lesson, I helped him move the furniture away from the walls so we'd be ready first thing.

Before I leave, Mom kisses me, then says she's going to take a long hot shower.

I'm locking my apartment door when Royce races down the steps. He's got on a Brooklyn Nets jersey and a new pair of sneakers.

"Man, where you been?" He sighs in disapproval. "I put in a good word for you and you don't show up?"

I try handing him the phone. "I changed my mind. I don't want anything to do with Andre or his business."

His hands shoot toward the ceiling like I'm about to rob him. "No way, I put my rep on the line for you. You have to do it now."

I never asked him to put his reputation out there for me. It was nice to know he thought I could handle it, but that's not going to make me change my mind. "I'm not doing anything."

He tilts his head to the side. "You trying to make me look stupid in front of Andre?"

"No," I say.

"I get it. You scared, right?" His attitude is gone.

I nod. "Aren't you? You saw those guys in the Charger."

"Yeah, I am and I really don't want to do any of this either."

"Then why're you doing it? You should just tell Andre to find somebody else."

"I'm planning just one more delivery and then I'm gone. It's happening later, and Andre's coming with me."

"So, why do you need me?"

"Andre wants a third person close by, kind of like a lookout. It's something his uncle taught him from back in the day."

"A lookout for what?"

Royce takes a deep breath. "For anything that doesn't seem right."

"None of this is right, so . . ."

I follow as Royce walks to the hallway window.

The courtyard is empty except for Mr. Brown reading a newspaper on one of the benches. His long, skinny brown legs stretch out before him. Today he's wearing a tan Kangol with a brown stripe down the middle.

"I know, I know," Royce whispers. "I mean like the police."

"The police. Are you kidding?"

"Yeah, but don't worry. Andre says that probably won't happen. Plus, it's not like you'll even be that close to us. You'll have a code word and if you do see them, all you'll have to do is yell it out so we can hear you."

It doesn't sound like I could get into trouble for just saying a word but I'm still not sure, so I don't know how to answer.

We don't say anything for a while, and then Royce clears his throat. "We need the money."

Who doesn't? I want to ask, but the seriousness in his voice tells me not to, so I just listen quietly.

"My mom used to be the bookkeeper at that club down on Atlantic Avenue. They fired her because she wouldn't do . . . man, never mind. She just doesn't work there anymore and I'm glad. But eventually, things started getting tighter, and my mom was having trouble paying for her asthma medicine. You just can't go without breathing, you know? So when Andre offered, I was in."

I can't even remember when things weren't tight for me and Mom. I know needing a new pair of shoes isn't the same as needing medicine. But I wish Mom didn't have to keep wearing her old beat-up ones. "I hear you."

It starts raining and Mr. Brown makes a run for it into his building.

"It's just going to be this one time, like I told you." Royce turns to me and I can plainly see the desperation in his eyes. It looks like he might start crying. "You should hear what my mom sounds like when she's having trouble breathing." He pauses. "It's like she's trying to suck air through a tiny straw. She doesn't have anybody else, so it's up to me to take care of her."

I feel really bad about his mom but I'm still having a hard time deciding. "I don't know . . ."

"C'mon, please? If you don't do it, the only other person is Tyke and what if he messes up again and we get caught?"

"Um . . ."

"I know you're worried about the police but you don't have to be. If by some chance they do come around, Andre's uncle said they hardly ever pay attention to the lookouts. Most likely they'll only want Andre."

"Or you," I say.

Royce shakes his head. "Not as much as Andre. Look, I could really use a friend right now. It won't take long at all. Ten minutes, if that."

I want to help him but I need to know more. "What else did Andre's uncle say about lookouts?"

Royce perks up like I've already said yes. "He said a lookout is like the tail of a snake to the police; they don't really matter. It's the head they want. So if you ask me, it's Andre who should really worry."

I might be wrong but that all makes sense to me. "Okay, but it'll be just this once."

"Yo, thank you. It means a lot," he says.

"But take the cell," I add. "I won't need it. Just tell me where and when, and I'll be there." Once again, I don't have a clue how I'm going to get away from my mom, Miss D., and Mr. Owen without a whole lot of questions, but I'm hoping I'll come up with something.

He takes the cell this time. "Twelve o'clock, across the street from the basketball court. Andre's picking me up, so I'll meet you there."

I check my watch. That's an hour from now. "What's the code word?"

"Rebound."

He's just about to leave when his cell rings. "Hey, Ma. Okay, I'll be right there."

He walks back toward the staircase. "I have to help my mom with something. I'll see you later. Don't forget, twelve o'clock."

Once inside Miss D.'s, we get right to work.

"This is how you do it," Mr. Owen says, filling a tray with paint, then running a roller through it.

The windows are wide open and there's newspaper already laid out on the floor. A tall fan is set up in the corner to help dry the paint. "First you make a 'W' like this." A big yellow "W" covers Miss D.'s wall. "Then you spread it evenly into a square. You just keep doing that over and over until the wall is done."

Getting closer to him, I sniff the air dramatically. "Wait, what's that smell?" I tease.

"Oh, you like that?" he says, straightening his already straightened collar. "It's sandalwood. Miss D. says I smell earthy and strong."

I explode with laughter.

He hands me the roller. "That's quite enough out of you."

When I'm done with my "W," he says, "Looks good." Then he gives me a couple of damp rags. "You'll need these for wiping up any paint drips. Go on and get started, son. I'll be back in a minute."

He's never called me "son" before. It makes me think

he really cares about me and that feels good. I get started and accidentally sling some paint across my pants. The rags don't help much. The more I try to wipe it, the worse it gets.

In the kitchen, Mr. Owen and Miss D. are talking but their words are too low to make anything out. Every once in a while, though, they laugh loud and hard and I wonder what's so funny.

I check the time. I've only got thirty minutes before I have to meet up with Royce, and I still haven't come up with an excuse to leave.

To save time, I skip the "W" thing but I still only finish one wall before Mr. Owen comes in wearing a silly smile.

"What's so funny?" I ask.

"Dotty sure has a sense of humor."

"Dotty?" I stop in mid-roll. "Nobody ever calls her that. You two are pretty serious, huh?"

"You sure left a lot of holidays," he says, ignoring my question.

I check my watch. "Holidays?"

"Step back from the wall and you'll see what I'm talking about."

There are lots of spots I completely missed with the paint. Most of them are small but some are big. "You mean the places I can still see the old paint?"

"Yep. It's like you took a break, or as I like to call it, a holiday, while you were in the middle of painting."

I dip the roller into the paint again and go over what I missed.

Mr. Owen takes a brush and starts slowly painting around the window.

I peek at my watch again. I need to be there in ten minutes. If I don't go now, right now, I won't make it on time and Royce will be out there with no one looking out for him. He's counting on me.

"Mr. Owen," I say, deciding to tell him the truth. "One of my friends is going to need my help in a few minutes. You think I can go? I promise to come right back," I quickly add.

Mr. Owen doesn't say anything. He just goes on painting around the window. He doesn't get a drop on the glass and I can't help but think it's a good thing he's doing it and not me. Finally he says, "And which friend would that be?"

Upbeat music pours in from the living room. Miss D. is playing the piano and I'm not surprised when she starts singing. It sounds like she's having a good time too.

Now, I think about lying but don't. "Royce."

Grab your coat and get your hat.
Leave your worries on the doorstep.
Life can be so sweet on the sunny side of the street.

Mr. Owen stops his brush mid-stroke. "Hey now, she's playing my kind of music." He starts bopping along. "My mother and father played her records out! Man, I heard

Ella Fitzgerald's music so much around my house I had no choice but to learn to love it."

That makes me think of Lionel Richie, but I don't exactly love him the way Mr. Owen seems to love this Ella Fitzgerald. I have to admit, though, her music is kind of catchy even if it's old-fashioned. And it's a lot of fun watching Mr. Owen as he bounces in rhythm to the music. He even snaps along.

I start bopping too, but it's not because of the music. I've got to leave. "So, can I?"

A smile stretches across his thoughtful brown face. "First lady of song, Miss Ella Fitzgerald, sing it if you please."

"Mr. Owen, can I please go help Royce?"

Loud noises suddenly fill the air outside. *Pop, pop, pop, pop.*

Mr. Owen drops down to the floor. His smile collapses, eyes narrow. "Get down," he hisses. "Those were gunshots!"

16

My legs won't move. They lock into place and it's only after Mr. Owen pulls me down by my wrist that I hit the soft carpet.

"William!" Miss D. calls, panicked, from the living room.

Mr. Owen orders me away from the window and into the corner. Then he rushes to join Miss D. "Dotty, move away from the windows and get down on the floor!"

I rush into the corner as fast as I can.

A girl is yelling outside. "They're shooting on Columbia Street!"

When I hear that, I'd rather be with Mr. Owen and Miss D., so I crawl into the living room.

They're on their knees by the couch. Mr. Owen helps Miss D. put a pillow underneath her legs. When I reach them, the three of us huddle together. *Pop, pop, pop.*

The noise is closer than before and my whole body trembles. I wrap my arms around my knees as tightly as possible. Then I try concentrating only on the rain, which has really started coming down.

Miss D. moans softly, then says, "Oh, Lord!"

Mr. Owen takes her hand. "We'll be just fine. Don't you worry."

In the hallway, people pound up and down the steps, and I hope they know to stay away from the windows.

Suddenly, a loud voice. "Batten down the hatches!"

"That's Santiago," Mr. Owen says. "What's he doing?"

His voice moves farther away. "All hands on deck!"

"Why's he saying that? What does it mean?" I say.

"He's having one of his episodes." Mr. Owen stands, but not to his full height. "Lionel, I'll stop by your apartment first to let your mother know all is well up here, then go after Santiago. I'll be back as soon as I can."

Now I see exactly why they gave Mr. Owen that medal. I doubt I could ever be that brave.

I slide over to Miss D. and I'm happy when she hugs me. Maybe Mr. Owen had to bring Mr. Santiago to his apartment, because he doesn't come right back. It must be a nightmare living like Mr. Santiago—only knowing what was and not what is.

After a few minutes Miss D. says she thinks it'll be okay to get off the floor. I listen for sounds in the hallway but there aren't any. "I think so too."

I help her to her chair but she doesn't relax into it. She sits on the edge like she's about to get up any minute.

"Miss D., do you want a glass of water or something?"

She gives a smile but it's gone in a blink. "No, thank you,

sweetheart." She points to my pants. "Your mother isn't going to be too happy with that paint on your jeans."

"Yeah, probably not."

But she's not paying any attention to me.

"Don't worry," I say after a minute. "Mr. Owen probably
just had to walk Mr. Santiago to his apartment. You want me
to go check? It's only one floor up."

When Miss D. gets up to peek out of the window, her legs
make a cracking noise just like when I crack my knuckles.

"The rain has stopped," she says. "And the courtyard
does seem to have settled down."

"Okay, I'll go check, then."

I knock hard and loud on Mr. Santiago's door but no one
answers. Inside it's silent. I should go tell Miss D., but that'll
only make her more nervous than she already is. I run down
to the first floor, then out into the mostly empty courtyard,
looking for Mr. Owen.

Nelson is at the window of his third-floor apartment.
Even though I don't want to talk to him, I ask if he's seen Mr.
Owen. The only answer I get is a slammed window. I can't
say that I blame him, but I yell up to him anyway.

"Forget you, Nelson! I don't need you."

Even if he had left his window open, there's no way he
would've heard me over the sirens that have just started
wailing.

I rush out of the courtyard but still no sign of Mr. Owen.

I get to the basketball court on Columbia Street just as three police cars and four ambulances pull up in front of a crowd.

When I get a closer look, I wish I had stayed in Miss D.'s apartment working on my holidays.

There's a car parked in the middle of the action with all the doors flung open.

I've been in that car.

It's black.

It's got cool rims.

Tinted windows too.

All I can think about is Royce. He could be in that car. Andre's car.

I feel like the blood drains out of my head. Two more police cars drive up and when the officers hop out, they try to push the crowd farther back, but we only move a little.

One of the policemen goes off to the side and talks to a kid who says he saw the whole thing.

I'm relieved when I spot Mr. Owen kneeling over someone not too far from the driver's door of Andre's car. But I'm scared too because something about the tint of the puddle near Mr. Owen tells me it's more than just water.

Inching closer, I get a better look at what Mr. Owen is doing. His clothes are soaked and his forehead glistens with tiny beads of water. The nearby puddle is a pool of blood. I try telling myself it's fake but I know it's not.

I think about how instead of running from something

dangerous, Mr. Owen ran toward it. I guess he always has. This might be silly, but I feel proud of him. When Mr. Owen stands, letting a paramedic with long dreads take his place, I see that it's Andre lying on the ground. One of the guys from Andre's crew is sitting next to him bleeding from his shoulder. As a paramedic helps him, he stares off into space like he's in shock. I panic. That means Royce is here somewhere and if I had met up with him the way I was supposed to . . . maybe I'd be lying on the ground too.

Frantically, I make my way through the crowd. "Royce?"

That's when I finally see Mr. Santiago. He seems fine now. He's talking to a man I've never seen before.

Another paramedic goes to the passenger side of the car. I push through the crowd to see what she's going to do. Little Tyke is on the ground moaning. He looks smaller than ever. Blood has soaked through the leg of his pants. The paramedic goes to work on him right away.

A woman lets out a long scream and it almost sounds like another siren. Then she pushes past us. "Tyke? Where's my son?"

"Ma?" Tyke says, trying to look past the paramedic.

Tyke isn't my friend, and after hitting me, he probably never will be, but I don't want him to be hurt. He's just a kid, the same as me. A tall blond policeman takes Tyke's mom by the elbow and moves her away from the car. His voice is calm, like maybe he's giving driving directions to someone instead of standing in the middle of this craziness. "The paramedic is taking care of him. It's best if you stay with me, ma'am."

When Tyke's mother starts crying hysterically, the policeman puts his arm over her shoulders and they walk a few feet away.

I spend a couple of minutes scanning the crowd for Royce, but he's nowhere around.

The paramedics wheel Andre into an ambulance first, then Tyke and the other guy into two others. Mr. Owen sees me and slowly makes his way over. His hands and shirt are stained with Andre's blood and I can't stop looking at it. "Lionel," he says, out of breath. "I wanted you to stay at Miss D.'s. You shouldn't be here."

"I'm sorry, but Miss D. was starting to worry about you," I say. "Have you seen Royce?"

"No, I haven't. Let's get back to Miss D.'s."

We start walking and Mr. Owen stumbles but doesn't fall. "I need to slow down."

"Why, what's wrong?" I say.

"I'm feeling a little dizzy." He puts his hand on my shoulder.

"Do you want to sit somewhere?" I ask, looking around for a place.

"No, no, it'll pass. Let's just get back to Miss D. We've got that room to finish painting."

We start to walk again but stop when Mr. Owen stumbles again. "Are you okay?" I ask.

But when he looks at me I know he isn't. His eyebrows draw together and his lips press tightly like he's in pain. I ask again.

"I . . . I'm not sure . . ."

"What do you mean?"

He grabs his arm. "Lionel . . ."

I try holding him up but he falls to his knees anyway.

"Mr. Owen!" I look around for help.

I hold him by his shirt but he slips out of my hands and goes down hard, hitting the side of his face.

"Help!" I say, getting on the ground next to Mr. Owen. "Somebody please help!"

The crowd rushes over to us and begins to ask questions.

"Is that William Owen?"

"Did he fall?"

"What's wrong with him?"

I touch Mr. Owen's face. His lips are purple and his eyes are open but I don't think he can see. This isn't right. He just helped save somebody's life and now he's lying on the ground like he's a victim too.

A paramedic from the fourth ambulance pushes through the crowd. "What happened?" she says, checking Mr. Owen's pulse.

"I don't know. He just fell. You have to help him!"

The paramedic calls for her partner, her voice booming. "Michele, we need a shock box over here!"

Her partner, red-faced and grim, hurries over carrying an orange duffel bag and something the size of a laptop. It has a handle, a screen, and some buttons. Michele quickly opens the bag and pulls out a pair of scissors, but it's not a regular one. The blades on this one bend upward and almost look like the letter L. "Faint pulse." She cuts open Mr. Owen's shirt, and with a wad of gauze, wipes his chest.

A ripple of fear shoots through my body like tiny lightning bolts. I lean in, letting the scent of his cologne wash over me. In a flash, I see him smiling big and goofy, the way he did when he told me how much Miss D. likes it.

Shaking his shoulder, I howl, "Mr. Owen! Please, wake up!"

I expect him to ask why I'm yelling, but he doesn't. He only lies in the spot where he fell, silent and still.

In a strange way, I feel like everything is far away and out of reach. Like I'm watching through a small window made of thick scratchy glass.

"Oh, my God," Mom says, suddenly standing beside me. Anisa is with her.

Anisa's voice cracks. "Lionel?"

Together we watch as Michele attaches two round pads, which are connected to the shock box, to Mr. Owen's chest. Then she flips a switch and a little green light starts to flash. "Clear!"

Mr. Owen's upper body lifts off the ground just a little, and for a minute I let myself believe that he's moving on his own and soon he'll sit up and wonder why we're all staring at him. When Michele says "Clear" again, I know that won't happen.

We listen to the third "Clear," then wait for a miracle.

17

It's Monday and Mom and I take Miss D. home after the funeral. I hesitate at the door like a high diver at the edge of a diving board. Going inside will only make me think of the last time I was here with Mr. Owen. Mom takes my hand and we go in together.

Mom settles Miss D. in her recliner, then goes into the kitchen to make her something to eat, even though Miss D. says she's not hungry.

"Just a little something. You haven't eaten well in the last two days and that's not good."

I sit on the couch across from Miss D. but she doesn't seem to notice me. It's probably better that way, because I'm afraid if our eyes meet, I'm going to start crying and never stop.

A heart attack. Mr. Owen had a heart attack. Miss D. said his passing was probably quick, and I wish I could believe her, but it didn't seem that way to me. Everywhere I look, I see Mr. Owen as clear as if he's standing in front of me, showing off his boxing skills or teaching me how to play cards. I close my eyes but it doesn't help.

I check out a photo of Miss D.'s son on the table beside the couch. I think about how nobody knew where to find Mr. Owen's son. He doesn't even know his dad is gone. If my father died and I didn't get the chance to see him one last time, I might go insane. That makes my head throb and I know where the tightness in my throat will lead, so I excuse myself and go into the bathroom. I splash cold water from the sink onto my face. Once, twice, three times, but no amount of water can stop the tears from coming.

Back in the living room, Mom is just setting up Miss D.'s lunch tray. One look at me and she knows I've been crying. She hugs me tightly before telling me to go home. I'm glad because I don't want Miss D. to see me so upset. She's got enough of her own hurt.

Once inside my apartment, I put my father's shirt on and go right to bed. I have a hard time sleeping, but when Mom gets in a long while later, I pretend to be knocked out. I'm not in the mood to talk and Mom isn't even in the mood for Lionel Richie.

I sleep through breakfast, and when my eyes open, it takes me a couple of seconds to remember that we buried Mr. Owen yesterday. The only place for me today is this bed. I must doze off, because when I wake up again, Mom is sitting on the side of my bed watching me. Even in my unlit room, it's easy to tell she's as sad as I feel.

"I'm taking a few days off work." Her voice is quiet and calm.

I nod, happy to know she'll be home with me. "Been over to Miss D.'s this morning. She's in pretty bad shape. Only got up to use the bathroom and that's it. Won't eat much and didn't have a lot to say."

She puts her hand on my cheek. "How about you? Are you okay?"

Mom leans in, watching me closely. Her eyes are full of concern.

I shrug, knowing if I try talking about it—about Mr. Owen falling and dying right in front of me—I'll sob myself back to sleep.

Mom understands because she doesn't ask again. She just kisses my forehead and sits with me for the longest time.

I don't get up to brush my teeth or even wash my face. I spend the whole day in bed like I've got the flu, only eating the buttered toast Mom brings me around dinnertime.

The next day, about an hour after Mom gets in from Miss D.'s, she calls softly through my bedroom door, where I'm still lying in bed, "Lionel, Anisa's here."

Unlike yesterday, at least I've brushed my teeth. Nothing else, though. I haven't even thought about Anisa, Eva, or the baby.

It takes Anisa a few seconds to adjust to the darkness. Finally she whispers, "Are you all right?"

My voice is raspy. "I don't know."

"Me either," she says. "They found the guys who did it and I hope they go to jail forever."

It's good that they caught them, but that can't bring Mr. Owen back. "I hope so too."

I sit up and move closer to the wall so she can sit. "How's Eva and the baby—I mean Angelina?"

"Eva's out of the hospital and has to go to court in a few days. The lawyer is walking Eva and my mother through everything. Child Services interviewed all of us and even came to our apartment to see where we live. They were really nice and helped us fill out a bunch of forms. If all the paperwork goes through, and the judge is satisfied, they said Angelina will be home soon."

"What did your mom do to Eva?" I ask, thinking about how when Mom was pregnant with me, she got screamed at for a month and then not spoken to at all.

"She was madder than I've ever seen. She stripped Eva's room bare. Took out her television and computer and boxed up her books. When she saw the dog-eared college book on Eva's desk, she sat on the floor and broke down."

I never thought I'd feel bad for Anisa's mom but I do now.

"Will you come see the baby after she's home?" Anisa says.

"Your mom would probably kill me if I ever set foot in your house again."

"No, she wouldn't, Lionel. Ms. Lugo, the councilwoman, has been helping us like you wouldn't believe, especially my mom. Between my aunt Doris and Ms. Lugo, they got her to realize that if it wasn't for your help, Eva could've died. Don't be surprised if my mom even thanks you."

I laugh for the first time in four days. "Yeah, right," I say.

She hits my shoulder playfully. "For real."

Things get quiet again until she says, "Does your eye hurt?"

"Not so much anymore. The color is getting better too. How's your leg?"

"Getting better." She shakes her head sadly. "I'm gonna miss seeing Mr. Owen around here, you know?" I nod. She's silent for a minute, then says, "Why did he have to die?"

"I don't know." My words come out shaky. "I'm going to miss him so . . ." My throat tightens too much to finish.

"I'll never forget how he looked lying there in the street." Anisa takes a deep breath, then says, "Eva and the baby could be dead too. I just . . ." Anisa covers her face, then bursts into tears like she's been holding them in the whole time.

All I can think to do is hug her.

We stay that way for a few minutes before Anisa asks for a tissue. I go into the bathroom and grab a couple. I take some for myself too.

When she blows her nose, I let out a tiny laugh.

She stops mid-blow. "What?"

"You sound like the Staten Island Ferry blowing its horn."

She smiles weakly, then we fall into a comfortable silence.

I lie back down again but Anisa tries pulling me up. "Oh, no, you don't. You have to get up even if it's just for a little while. It'll be good for you, Lionel." She continues to tug even though I haven't moved an inch. "Let's go visit Miss D. I bet she'd be happy to see you."

That almost gets me going but my body just won't do it. "Maybe we can go tomorrow."

Anisa tries to get me to talk some more but I'm too tired. She sits with me a little while longer, then leaves.

Even though Mom checks in on me, sits on my bed, and rubs my back, I feel alone.

A heaviness in my chest weighs me down. I can barely walk to the kitchen table to eat, and when I do, chewing is too much work, so I don't eat much. I'm not very hungry anyhow.

I spend most of the day thinking about my father and Mr. Owen. I know for a fact that if Mr. Owen had a choice he would've never left. Just like Anisa's father wouldn't have left. But my father left and never looked back.

Mom comes in to kiss me good night just before I fall asleep. I even let her tuck me in like I'm five years old.

• • •

In the morning when Mom comes in, her thick hair in a high ponytail. She's wearing an old pair of jeans and a black T-shirt with bleach stains. She's carrying a pair of work gloves, a shovel, and a big water jug. She plops everything down on the floor like her arms just can't carry them anymore. It's the most noise I've heard in days.

"It's Thursday, it's time," she says, pulling up the blinds.

Sunlight fills my room. The light hurts my eyes and I shield them like I'm a vampire. I lift the covers over my face.

Mom says, "I don't think so." She throws them to the floor, leaving me in my sleep shorts and my father's shirt.

"No, Mom . . ."

She moves closer to my bed and I get a better look at the bags underneath her eyes. "Losing Mr. Owen has been very tough. Please, Lionel," she says. "You've been in bed since Monday afternoon and it's not good for you." Her voice is unsteady, like she's having a hard time keeping the words from knotting up in her throat.

She wipes her tears with the bottom of her stained shirt and I remember that she's been left too. I reach for her hand and let her pull me out of bed.

"Nothing can take away the time you and Mr. Owen spent together." She hugs me and I smell her face lotion, which smells like coconut. It comforts me, reminding me of the sunscreen Mom used to put on me when we spent the day at Coney Island. "Take hold of those times, Lionel," she continues. "The ones that make you smile and feel good, and never, never let them go."

We stay that way for a long time. Then, looking to the things she came in with, I say, "So, what's up with that stuff?"

"Get ready. We're planting a tree in Mr. Owen's memory today."

18

I wash up and get dressed in record time. Then Mom asks me to fill a jug with water.

We take the elevator up to Miss D.'s, and when we get off, I make sure not to look at Mr. Owen's apartment.

Miss D. opens her door after just one knock. She's wearing a brown dress with long fringe hanging from the cuffs. Her white hair is parted down the middle with a braid on each side and she's wearing the peace sign earrings Mr. Owen gave her. She seems close to her regular self, only her smile isn't a true Miss D. smile. I can't even see her teeth but I'm happy for it anyway.

"I'm so glad to see you, Lionel."

I kiss her on the cheek. "Hi, Miss D."

"You all set, Miss D.?" Mom asks.

"Yes, I am," she says, stepping out into the hallway and locking her door.

"We could not have asked for a nicer day," Mom says once we're on the elevator.

Miss D. fidgets with her earring. "Maybe William had something to do with it. He was a charmer . . ."

"Yes, he was," Mom says. Outside our building, leaning against the bench, is a skinny tree with baby leaves. There's a bunch of people gathered near it. The roots of the tree are wrapped in burlap and tied with twine. Not too far from the tree is a covered plastic bin on wheels. The sturdy kind you get at Home Depot.

Mr. Santiago doesn't seem confused about where he is, because he's talking calmly to Mr. Brown, Anisa, Dellie, Mrs. Torres, and Bella. "William would sure get a kick out of having his own tree," he says.

Everyone says good morning, including Anisa's mom. She and Mom even exchange smiles.

"Mr. Santiago, will you take the tree to the spot?" Miss D. asks.

"Surely."

Everyone is quiet as we follow, even Bella.

Mr. Santiago walks to the middle of what used to be a grassy area not too far from our building. Now it's mostly dirt.

"This spot will do just beautifully," Miss D. says, looking toward the sun, then to me. "Will you do the honors?"

Miss D. directs me on how deep and wide the hole needs to be.

Before I get started, Mom puts her arm over my shoulders and gives me a squeeze.

"Wait!" we hear just as I stab the tip of the shovel into the dirt.

It's Eva and she's carrying a small pink bundle. Angelina!

"*Cuidado!* Careful," Anisa's mom calls out.

"Don't worry, Mami," Eva says.

When Eva reaches us, we crowd around her. The baby is wearing a pink dress and a floppy white hat. Anisa's mom adjusts the brim so we can see Angelina's face better. She's asleep and doesn't seem to mind the chatter that has just started going on around her.

"Oh, she's beautiful," Mom says. "Congratulations, Eva."

Miss D. looks over Eva's shoulder. "My goodness gracious, isn't she just as sweet as pie?"

"Heaven is most definitely missing an angel," Mr. Santiago says.

Three-year-old Bella wants to see the baby too, so Dellie picks her up. "Isn't the baby cute?" Dellie says.

"My baby!" Bella says, laughing.

Even Mr. Brown gushes. "My Loretta's going to love hearing all about this little princess."

I want to say something too but I don't know what. I'm feeling too many things at once, making it hard to speak.

Anisa walks over to me and smiles. Her eyes are shiny with happy tears and that's when I realize mine are too. I guess we don't need to say anything.

"Lionel," Eva says, looking past everyone, her face serious. "Thank you."

That's when Anisa's mother does something surprising. She kisses my cheek. *"Muchas gracias."*

Mom grins bigger than I've seen in a while.

"You're welcome," I say.

Then Anisa's mom hugs Eva like she'll never let go.

I remember how Mr. Owen said "community" like it was the most important word in the world and know it's the truth. I look around at everyone and feel so much love I think I might burst. After everything that we've been through, I know we'll be all right.

"Okay, everyone," Miss D. says. "Time to get planting."

It's not hard work and the July sun isn't even that hot yet, but with every shovelful, I think about Mr. Owen. It doesn't make me sad, it just makes me want to do a good job—no, a great job, because that's how Mr. Owen would do it.

After I'm done, Mr. Santiago unwraps the ball of roots, then sets the tree inside the hole.

"Okay, Lionel," Miss D. says. "Fill the hole back up, and be sure to flatten the soil down as best you can."

When the tree is standing on its own, Mr. Santiago removes something big from a shopping bag. It's a fake rock about the size of a thick dictionary. Attached to it is a plaque that reads

IN MEMORY OF MR. WILLIAM OWEN,

OUR BELOVED FRIEND AND NEIGHBOR.

Mr. Brown takes off his red and black Kangol. I've never seen him without a hat. His hair is curly and bright white.

Mr. Santiago kneels down in front of the tree, and using the attached metal spikes, he presses the rock into the dirt. He adjusts it a few times before getting it just right. He uses his handkerchief to wipe tears from his eyes before standing up. "This is a Yoshino cherry tree, one of Mr. Owen's favorites," Miss D. says. "Right now, it's a skinny little thing, but come next April, the flowers on this tree will be absolutely beautiful and pinker than pink.

"During the Cherry Blossom Festival in Washington, D.C., these trees are the main attraction. Did you all know William was born and raised in Washington?"

"I did," Mr. Brown says.

No one else says a word.

"Because of that," Miss D. continues, "I thought the Yoshino would be the perfect way to honor his life." She pauses for a minute to wipe her eyes with a crumpled tissue before going on. "Right here, in Red Hook, Brooklyn, where he was so loved."

Just then, Bella breaks away from Anisa and Dellie and twirls in a circle. With the hem of her dress flaring, she yells, "Loved!"

That makes us all laugh a little. Miss D. begins to speak again. "Though William has gone on to glory, I know that he is watching over us." She dabs her eyes again. "So for

William, I sing this song by his favorite singer, Miss Ella Fitzgerald."

I'll be there always
Not for just an hour, not for just a day
Not for just a year, but always.
I'll be loving you, oh, always
With a love that's true, always.

Miss D. is on the verge of breaking down. Her voice wobbles and she's only able to get through a little bit of the song.

For a couple of minutes the only sound coming from our group is sniffling.

Finally Miss D. says, "Lionel, will you water Mr. Owen's tree, please?"

I wish I had a tissue, crumpled or not. I use the back of my hand to wipe my eyes before the tears have a chance to wet my face.

I get right to work soaking the dirt around the tree. When I'm done I have the urge to touch the rock, so I do. It's warm from sitting in the sun and it's not as rough as I thought it would be. Looking up at the sky, I wonder what Mr. Owen would think of it if he could see it. Maybe he'd say, "That's mighty fine."

The next thing I know, everybody else lines up and touches the rock too.

"And now," Miss D. motions for my mother to uncover the plastic bin, "I'd like everyone to take one, two if there's enough to go around."

Water balloons!

"Wouldn't it be nice to have Mr. Owen's tree surrounded by beautiful flowers?" Miss D. asks.

Everyone nods in agreement but I don't think they have a clue what she means, so I fill them in. "There are seeds inside these balloons. All you have to do is throw them so they'll pop on the dirt and the flowers will grow!"

"Thank you, Mr. Richie," Miss D. says, beaming.

I mirror her smile, glad to be of help.

Eva and the baby move far away before we get started.

Anisa is the first to go and of course she chucks one right by my feet. I return the favor. Before long, everyone is a little muddy with wet feet and legs.

After we're done, and the area empties out, it's my job to stay behind and collect the popped balloons. Miss D. says if a bird or dog gets hold of them, they'll choke to death or get really sick.

I'm just about done when Royce approaches. It's been five days since I've seen him last.

"Hey, Lionel, what's up? You feel like shooting some hoops?"

"Hoops? Are you serious? After everything that's happened?"

Royce breaks eye contact and looks around. Then he eases his hands into the pockets of his jeans. "I know, man." His voice is soft. "I'm sorry, I just didn't know what else to say to you."

"It's okay," I say, knowing he really means it. "So where were you when everything happened? I tried looking for you."

"Remember when we were talking in the hallway and my mom called me back upstairs?"

I nod.

"Well, her asthma was acting up, and she needed me to stay with her in case it got really bad."

"Well, that was lucky," I say.

"Yeah, and I'm never ever getting mixed up in stuff like that again. My mom needs me too much."

I know just what he means. My mom might not have trouble breathing but we do need each other. Miss D. needs us too.

"She's set with her asthma medicine now, though, at least for a little while."

"That's good, but how?"

"You didn't hear?" Royce's grin is big and proud. "I won Enzo's pinball tournament and the five hundred bucks!"

I can't believe I missed it. When Enzo told me and Anisa about it, he wasn't even sure when it was going to be. At least the money went to a good cause, though. I shake his hand. "Congrats, man. That's awesome."

"Thanks." Royce motions toward Mr. Owen's tree. "So, what's this all about?"

"We planted it for Mr. Owen."

"Oh." He studies the writing on the plaque. "Tyke was lucky. He never came close to dying but Mr. Owen saved Andre's life."

"He did." I think about Mr. Owen's medal. "He saved lots of lives in Vietnam."

"Serious?"

I nod. "He was the bravest person I've ever known."

After three weeks of searching the Internet at the library, Mr. Santiago finally tracks down Thomas, Mr. Owen's son.

Early one Saturday morning, Miss D. calls to tell us that Thomas has come to empty out Mr. Owen's apartment. Mom and I go up and knock on Mr. Owen's door.

Mom introduces herself, then me. He hardly looks at us when he says hello. Thomas is worn-out with tired eyes and deep creases on his face. One of his bottom teeth is missing and he's got a neck tattoo. I can't make out what it is because his shirt collar is in the way.

Just like Mr. Owen, he has dark skin and poked-out ears. "We wanted to give our condolences. Your father and Lionel spent some time together." Mom pats my back.

"I know," Thomas says. "Miss D. told me."

"Well, he was a wonderful man and will be greatly missed," Mom says.

Thomas replies with a cold "Thanks." Then he slips quietly back inside the apartment.

A couple of hours later, I go up to Miss D.'s and see Thomas at the garbage chute with some of Mr. Owen's things. Right away I get that weird feeling in my stomach I get when I'm just about to take a test. Only it's bigger, like a midterm or final.

Trying to identify the things he's holding, I quickly ask, "Did you find the letter your dad put away for you? He would've mailed it but he didn't know where to send it."

His shoulders slump and he stops mid-throw.

I hope I didn't say too much. Maybe he'll tell me to mind my business.

"Yeah, why? He told you what he wrote or something?"

I think about how sad Mr. Owen was when he told me he had no idea where his son was. "No, it just sounded important, that's all."

"Maybe at one time it was, but it was a little on the late side, you know what I mean?" He goes back to throwing away what's left of Mr. Owen's stuff.

He doesn't know how lucky he is. If I ever found something my father put away for me, I think I'd be happy. "Better late than never, right?" I say weakly.

"Maybe," he says, stopping to look at what he'll throw out next. "You know what? You should probably keep this," he says, holding Mr. Owen's medal.

"Really?" I say, not believing that he wouldn't want to keep it. "Your dad was a hero," I add. "You sure you don't want it?"

Thomas examines the frame for a couple of seconds before handing it over. "He used to be my hero a long, long time ago." His eyes are wet. "In another lifetime."

Finally he places the medal into my hands. He gives his eyes a fast wipe with the sleeve of his shirt, then says, "Take care of it, okay?"

The hardness about him falls away, letting me see somebody much younger—somebody who needed his father as much as I do.

"Thank you," I say.

Mr. Owen's deck of cards is next to be tossed out. "Can I have those too?"

"Sure. Is there anything else you want?"

"No, that's okay. I'll just take these. I'll give them to Miss D. Thanks," I say, turning away.

"Hey," he says. "Where's your father?"

"I have no idea."

"Then I'm glad my father was there for you," he says, studying me the same way Mr. Owen used to.

"So am I."

I wait for Thomas to knock on our door asking for Mr. Owen's stuff back. To say he's made a big mistake and to beg me for them. But he doesn't. I'm sad Mr. Owen didn't have his son all these years, but I'm sad for Thomas too.

I promise myself that if there's any way I can help it, I won't let that happen to me and my father.

As soon as I decide this, I feel lighter.

19

Dear Dad,

I'm not sure if you'll ever get this letter, but there are some things I need to put down on paper anyway.

I was only seven when you left. I didn't know a whole lot of things back then but I knew how much I loved you and I thought you loved me too.

After you went away, I felt hurt and unwanted. I thought you leaving was my fault. I kept thinking you would come back but you never did. I couldn't understand why I wasn't good enough to make you stay in the first place.

Living without you made me feel lopsided and incomplete, like trying to walk with only one leg. I felt alone even when I was with Mom.

Because of how I felt, I tried doing some really stupid things. I almost got mixed up with the wrong people, and I did something that could've gotten me into big trouble. I tried to steal an abandoned baby from a hospital. I thought if I could get the baby back to her mom, I could prevent her from feeling unimportant. I didn't want her to feel worthless and unloved too. I wanted her to be happy.

I've learned some things, though. I understand now that I don't need you to make me feel loved and wanted and worthy, because I feel that way all on my own. I might not ever find out if you love me, but you should know that I'll keep the love I have for you in a safe place. If you ever come back to me, it'll be here waiting for you. Maybe then we'll be able to fill in the hole you made when you left.

Maybe you'll get to see the man I've become.

Love, your son,
Lionel

Acknowledgments

Like Lionel, I grew up in the Red Hook Projects, where my *community* played a very important role in my life. I was lucky enough to have had a real Miss D. back then, and her name was Miss Spencer. Just like Miss D., Miss Spencer also had a piano in her apartment. Unfortunately, I never asked for a lesson. Miss Spencer was like my second mom, and though she is no longer with us, I hope she realized how special she was.

There were others, of course—Miss Seed, Grandma Frieda, Miss Frieda, and Miss Beulah, to name a few. These women may not have known their impact on me, but it was there, and I'd like to say thank you. *Community* is, indeed, the most important word in the world. This is something Hattie Carthan knew all those years ago in her Bedford-Stuyvesant neighborhood. Her hard work can still be felt today. You can find out more about her here: www.nycgovparks.org/parks/B400/history.

As always, I would like to thank my family for putting up with me while writing this book. Not only for supporting me during my craziest days and nights, but for not disowning me! What would I do without you all?

A million thanks to my brilliant editor, Stacey Barney, for her amazing ability to dig beneath the surface of a story and bring to light the heart of it. I am truly grateful.

To my youngest nieces, Aiva and Louise (aka Weezie Woman), may you find and keep close your *communities*.

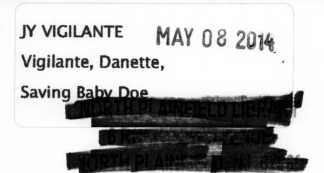